THEY'RE WATCHING

MICHAEL DAVID WILSON & BOB PASTORELLA

THIS IS HORROR

A This Is Horror Publication
www.thisishorror.co.uk

ISBN: 978-1-910471-05-0

Copyright © Michael David Wilson and Bob
Pastorella 2020
All rights reserved

The right of Michael David Wilson and Bob
Pastorella to be identified as the authors of this
work have been asserted by them in accordance with
the Copyright, Designs and Patents Act 1988.

First published in 2020 by This Is Horror

Editor: Max Booth III
Cover Art: Pye Parr
Design and Layout: Lori Michelle

This is a work of fiction. All characters and events
portrayed in this book are fictional, and any
resemblance to real people or incidents is purely
coincidental.

PRAISE FOR THE AUTHORS

PRAISE FOR MICHAEL DAVID WILSON

"Propulsive, modern, funny, frightening. *The Girl in the Video* will make you think twice about opening any anonymous videos sent your way. Then it'll make you think twice again. Michael David Wilson has long added to the genre with his incredible podcast/press This is Horror, but here he offers a book, and now it's time for someone else to interview him."

—Josh Malerman,
New York Times bestselling author of *Bird Box*

"*The Girl in the Video* took me somewhere I didn't want to go via a route I didn't want to take. It's an unsettling story of love, lust, and cultural disorientation that'll flirt with you and then, when you're at your most vulnerable, take full advantage of your good intentions."

—David Moody,
author of *Autumn* and *Hater*

PRAISE FOR BOB PASTORELLA

"If you're looking for a pulpy fast-paced southern-fried sleazed-out hard-boiled blast of bad drugs and weird crime, *Mojo Rising*'s got you covered in spades. Just go easy on the Mojo, alright? You open up the doors of perception, you never know who (or what) might break on through."

—Jeremy Robert Johnson,
author of *Skullcrack City*

PRAISE FOR THEY'RE WATCHING

"Feast your eyes, your heart, your deepest desires on Michael David Wilson and Bob Pastorella's *They're Watching*. It's fast, it's immersive, it lingers in your mind for days. This novel will not only leave you stranded in an awkward, breathless position wanting more, it will beg you to look closer, not just at the pages, but at that piece of your soul that wonders: is a secret really that bad if no one knows?"

—Mackenzie Kiera,
Ladies of the Fright* podcast and author of *All You Need is Love and a Strong Electric Current

"Michael David Wilson and Bob Pastorella have designed this highly entertaining and fast-moving thriller, an intricate little mind game with an unlikely hero and elements of both mystery and horror that will keep you guessing until the last page."

—S.P. Miskowski,
author of *I Wish I Was Like You*

"One of my favorite reads this year."

—Brennan LaFaro,
***Dead Headspace* podcast**

For all This Is Horror Podcast listeners.
Have a great great read.

ONE

THE FISH MOTIFS were jarring, but all in all Brian liked the way the apartments looked. The security gate and cameras mounted in the alcove gave him peace of mind, even though the thought of being watched unnerved him. The balconies were welcoming and spacious. Unlike his previous place they didn't resemble prison cells—the wrought iron bars, thick with rust, had suffocated him. The sinister fish statues scattered around the complex, with oddly angled fins and roaming eyes, served as a warning, telling thieves and burglars to stay away. The cameras for those who didn't heed their advice.

Most of Brian's belongings were scheduled to arrive later that afternoon. Impatient and curious, he needed to see his apartment, to check out the layout and visualise it with furnishings. The job was long-term even if the apartment was temporary, but Brian knew how easily temporary could become permanent once he settled into his comfort zone. He got out of his car—a maroon Ford Focus he'd owned almost a decade, banged-up but dependable—and checked he had the key in his pocket for the hundredth time.

A pretty woman—long black hair and large stylish sunglasses—rushed through the alcove to the pavement and headed to a car parked a few spaces from his.

Brian nodded at her. She barely smiled, flipped her ponytail at him. He tried not to stare. She was wearing rainbow yoga pants that left little to the imagination. No doubt that glimpse would give him something to think about later, after he'd settled in.

The complex was called Pelagic Court which was an improvement on Grey House in Birmingham, a place that lived down to its moniker. Inside, the apartment was larger than he'd expected and smelled brand new. Fortunately, the aquatic motifs that punctuated much of the buildings' exterior were absent inside. The furnishings were modern, with off-white walls and light blonde wooden cabinets. Brian pulled the safety strap off the fridge-freezer and opened the door. Two empty ice trays sat on the shelf. He reached for a tray but jumped back when he saw the cockroach on its back. Dark brown hair-covered legs raised up in the air. Brian prodded the bastard, checking it was dead, then pushed it into his hand, and lobbed it out of the window. He rinsed his hands, eyes peeled for other unwelcome visitors.

Brian filled the ice trays from the sink. The ice would go well with whiskey later. Once the movers dropped everything off, he'd want a drink, which reminded him he needed to stock up on essentials. Satisfied for the moment, Brian locked up, then located the closest supermarket on his smartphone, ignoring the distant music from a neighbouring apartment.

THEY'RE WATCHING

His new home was a small seaside town on the South Coast. Emphasis on *small*, it was a far cry from the Midlands where he'd been spoiled with a multitude of shops and pubs. Still, there was a big Sainsbury's a twenty-minute drive away, though Brian thought a forty-minute round-trip a bit much for a few provisions, so headed into the town centre to see what it offered. As luck would have it, there was a farmer's market every last Tuesday of the month. One stall had locally grown fruit and veg—ripe red tomatoes, deep green cucumbers, and apples bigger than Brian's fist. They let him look and touch without being too snotty.

Brian followed the crowd to the independent supermarket in the corner: 'Dylan & Son'. According to the sign it had been in business since 1912. If that many people were packing into a place so small it couldn't be too bad and it sure beat trekking out to Sainsbury's every time he ran out of bread. Things got off to a rocky start when some bearded bloke wearing a leather jacket and smelling of cigarettes and strong cologne bumped into Brian on his way out of the supermarket. Brian quickly helped him pick up his fallen shopping. They both made mumbled apologies and went their separate ways.

Whilst Brian was at the back of the shop looking for milk, he turned to see a tall man with an unkempt beard and long flowing red robe saunter down the aisle, shaking hands with everyone he approached, stopping for a few minutes to chat with some of the shoppers. Spicy incense perfumed the air. The guy smelt like one of those old goth emporiums that sold dragon figurines and pendants, legal highs and shisha, magic spells and so-called potions. Brian tried not to pay him any attention lest he get drawn into a conversation he didn't have time for. He pushed his trolley closer, avoiding eye contact with Red Robe.

"Now, don't trust . . . " but the conversation between Red Robe and the young couple petered out, as though they didn't want him to hear.

Perhaps it was just Brian's imagination because soon they were speaking again, saying their goodbyes. As Brian drew parallel, he looked up at Red Robe who quickly turned away. Spared an awkward conversation, Brian collected his milk and searched for the eggs.

➤╳◄

Brian got lost returning to the apartment—unable to shift the image of Red Robe parading up and down the aisles like a fucking celebrity—and ended up putting his address into the phone's SatNav. He didn't want to rely on it—and *hated* the robotic voice with its sickly sarcasm—but it was better than driving in circles. To top things off, a swift moving train caught him at a level crossing. By the time he made it home, the movers were waiting for him, their giant removal van backed close to the apartment's entrance. Brian left his things in the car whilst he unlocked the front door, grateful he was only on the first floor.

"You made it in record time," he told the driver—a gruff man with yellow teeth. He handed Brian the invoice to sign.

"Guess the rent here is high," the driver said, grinning like he knew something he wasn't sharing.

"Good thing my job pays well." Brian signed the paper, getting a whiff of stale cigarettes and body odour.

"Can't all be rich and stuck-up," the driver mumbled.

Stuck-up? Brian didn't say anything—he'd seen the size of the driver's biceps. His two skinhead colleagues were no layabouts either. Brian grabbed the groceries from the car and put them away. He got out of the way of the removal men and went for a wander around the block. There was a whole lot of nothing, but eventually he stumbled upon a corner shop where he picked up some beer for the removal men. He grabbed the cheapest crate he could find, not because of the money, but because he feared they'd think he was even more 'rich and stuck-up' if he bought the fancy stuff.

Back at the apartment, the lads appreciated it, busting open their cans and sucking foam from the top. Brian joined them, chugging a can of his own. He wasn't much of a beer man, but he had to admit it felt right drinking a few with these guys. On the way out the driver held back, whilst his colleagues rushed to the van. Brian stuffed his hands in his pockets. Was the driver waiting for an apology? Eventually Brian. relented.

"Listen, about earlier, I wasn't being a dick when I—"

The driver cast his hand aside. "Don't worry about it, mate. Water under the bridge and all that."

They continued to stare at each other. When the driver raised his hand to scratch his skull, Brian actually flinched. Brian then cleared his throat and scratched his own head as if the visual equivalent of autocorrect.

"It's just . . . " the driver said, then trailed off. "You'll be all right here, yeah?"

Now it was Brian's turn to look confused. "You've moved everything inside, so . . . "

"Of course, of course. You seem like a good kid is all." The driver backed towards the van. "Look after yourself and thanks for the beer."

The driver practically ran to his van, much as his colleagues had. Soon after, it bolted off down the road, leaving Brian alone on his doorstep.

Look after yourself . . . ?

Brian appraised the car park. His was the only vehicle. Where was the young lady he'd seen earlier? Maybe she didn't live here—probably the girlfriend of the other tenant.

And who *was* the other tenant? Brian imagined a young chap, blonde hair, total gym rat into his exercise. Maybe he'd return in the evening with Yoga Pants. Just how soundproof was the apartment? He'd heard music earlier and wondered if he'd hear the two of them going at it, shagging long into the night? The last place he'd lived the walls were practically rice paper, there'd been this young couple next door with a lot of stamina who believed louder sex was better sex.

Brian wandered into the kitchen where he poured himself a large Maker's Mark and cola, ready to call his sister, Helen. She'd been happy about his move: *a fresh start will be good for you. You need to get out more and mingle.* Not very subtle code for 'find a girlfriend and settle down for Christ's sake.' At any rate, Brian needed to tell her he'd made it down here safely but knew she'd have too many questions about everything and nothing. The thought of talking on the phone for hours when he had so much to do made him queasy. Helen meant well, loved him more than he likely deserved, but the whiskey provided a mild numbness, it took the edge off her constant badgering.

He was about to call when the folded scrap of paper was shoved through the door.

Brian opened it—blue ink on white paper. Two words: "Get Out."

Who the . . . ?

He opened the apartment door. "Hello?"

His voice echoed in the empty hall.

Brian rushed into the bedroom and peered out of the window. Whoever had left the note was either out of sight or in hiding. But who the hell would leave such a thing in the first place? And *why*?

"Get out . . . " He'd barely got in the damn place.

Brian rubbed his forehead. Perhaps it was a case of mistaken identity. Someone had had beef with an old tenant and left the note for them. Though Brian had thought the estate agent had said he was the first to live here—the dead cockroach in the fridge-freezer suggested otherwise. Perhaps the note had been meant for his neighbour? The mystery sender had posted it through the wrong door—a simple enough mistake to make. Still, Brian didn't fancy living in a place where people left passive-aggressive notes. And how did they get into the building in the first place? Wouldn't they need a key?

Brian puzzled over the matter a little longer until his laptop started singing in the living room. On Skype, Helen's display picture lit up the computer screen—side-parted golden locks teased her shoulders, light makeup, a soft smile. He quickly put on The Ocean's *Heliocentric*, grabbed the glass of Maker's Mark from the kitchen, and slouched back on the sofa—making as though he was having a good time and not shaken up from a vaguely threatening note, barely hours after moving in. He answered the call, deliberately selecting audio only as he scanned the living room for anything untoward. Mostly it was just cardboard boxes. Aside from the Bose speakers and whiskey glasses, Brian had yet to unbox anything, and he'd only unboxed them because he'd marked the packages appropriately: 'fragile' and 'important music shit'.

"Hey!" Helen's voice came through first, followed by her well-lit kitchen. She was chopping up vegetables, hair scrunched back in a bun, some pop hit playing in the background. "I was worried about you. Thought you'd have called by now."

He rubbed sleep out of his eyes, brushed a hand through his dishevelled hair, and turned on video.

"Sorry, I got distracted." Brian sat up straight on the sofa, forced a smile like 'hey, sis, everything's cool here, definitely not freaking out.'

Helen was frowning.

"It was a long drive down here," Brian said. "Then there were the removal men, shopping, checking out the neighbourhood. I've barely had time to sit down." He got up and started pacing the living room as if to make his point.

"It looks dark in there, everything okay?"

Brian turned on the light. The sun going down as the evening drew near. "See what I mean? So preoccupied I forgot to switch the lights on."

"But you're okay? You seem . . . distant."

"I'm tired, that's all. Nothing a good night's sleep won't fix."

The sound of a baby wailing in the background made Helen put the vegetable knife down and look off-camera. "It's okay, honey—shh, shh." As if by magic, Helen's words settled the kid. Brian wished his words were half as effective, these days he could barely get his subordinates to listen to him at work. It was just as well he'd been relocated and reassigned to a new department. A fresh opportunity to present himself as an employee who carried clout. Which he had to be, they weren't just going to move *anyone* from the Midlands down to the South Coast, especially when they'd taken care of much of the costs and kitted him out with a fancy new apartment.

"Gracie's not been sleeping well," Helen said. "She's teething."

Brian nodded. He didn't have much experience with children but knew enough parents with young kids to understand it was hard work. Gracie started wailing again, louder, more like caterwauling. *Guess Helen doesn't have the magic touch after all.*

"Sorry about this, I'd better go," she said. "But you *are* okay, *aren't* you?"

"I'm good, Helen. But what about you?"

She forced a smile. "Oh, you know me, I'm surviving. Keith will be round in a few hours to help with Gracie, so . . . "

Keith was Gracie's paternal grandfather and unlike his son, Mike, he was a constant in Gracie's life. Mike had bailed before Gracie's birth and as far as Brian understood, they'd barely spoken since. He knew the relationship had ended badly, though Helen had been vague with the details, and Brian had elected not to ask.

Brian closed the laptop. There was something about speaking with Helen that made him feel insignificant. She had the high-powered job, the fancy house, the nice car, and seemingly did everything from making a sandwich to defending a client to the highest standard. And all of this as a single mother, five years Brian's junior. Their parents, two years gone from this world, had always maintained they didn't have a favourite, but in Brian's mind the better of the siblings was glaringly obvious. He picked up the half-full whiskey glass and sank it, then poured himself another, this time straight, and sank that, too. *Get a hold of yourself, man. You're doing well, this move is your making, and you know it.*

He headed to the bedroom where he unpacked some of the basics: clothes, toiletries, towels and tea towels, bathroom products. But he lacked the energy and concentration to get much of it done. He flopped back on the bed and examined the 'Get Out' note. Brian told himself he was in control and drank whiskey until he believed it.

Re-energised, Brian resumed the music, this time opting for Mastodon's *Leviathan*, and began unpacking whilst thrashing his head to 'Blood and Thunder'.

Brian wasn't sure how long it took him to unpack the boxes in the living room but by the time he was done *Leviathan* was long over and his media player was selecting songs at random. There was a moment he thought his player was malfunctioning. As though two songs were playing at once. He muted his music, the other song's tempo now easier to hear. It came from next door. Strange, hypnotic music flowed softly from the walls.

His neighbours were finally home.

TWO

SOON BRIAN FOUND himself tapping away to the rhythm of the song. Its texture teasing him. He was in the presence of something special and longed to fully taste it. He followed the sound from living room to hallway where the tone was more prominent. Brian moved back and forth, searching for the optimum listening position. The open wardrobe blocked the wall, separating his and his neighbour's apartment.

Only one thing for it—he opened the door and leant inside, straining to hear.

A stack of towels blocked the back of the wardrobe. He pushed them aside, longing for a place to rest his ear—some of the tower of towels toppled over and flopped to the floor. He reached out to catch them but wound up smacking his right elbow against the metal hanging bar which struck the floor.

Expenses spared, huh?

Brian retrieved the bar and tried fixing it back in place when he noticed the piece where it connected to the wall was loose. He pressed it in, but it wouldn't budge. Prying his fingers underneath, Brian felt to see if there were nails holding the wall piece in position. As he dug deeper, the damn thing came off in his hands. It was nothing more than a painted piece of plasterboard. *Bloody hell!* He'd have to make a call to the estate agents first thing in the morning. There was no way the piece would stay up on its own, and he didn't have any nails, or even a hammer to set it back.

Then he noticed the peephole.

Light shining from it.

It gazed directly into his neighbour's apartment and was the exact size of his eyeball. As if someone had made it especially for him, and only him.

He peeked for a second, catching a silhouette, but was embarrassed, quickly turning away and stepping out of the open wardrobe. He was no creep. He put the towels back, concealing the hole and backing away.

In the living room, Brian examined the last of the unpacking, determined to finish even if it meant pulling an all-nighter. As he knifed open the tall cardboard box, the one with the fun stuff—CDs, DVDs, video games—all he could think about was that hole.

And the music continued to play.

Singing to him.

Imploring him.

Surely he could take a peek to see which room the hole peered into. If there was music, perhaps there was a party. He could grab a couple of beers and his best bottle of whiskey, knock on his neighbour's door, and introduce himself to a whole community of people. And if there was no party, well, he could see how his neighbour had kitted out the place—it might even provide him with some inspiration for furnishing his own pad. Ways to inject a bit of character. He pulled out a fat stack of DVDs. *Sleep Tight* stared back at him. On the cover, a single eye peeped through a crack in the door as an unclothed woman slept.

"What the hell is wrong with me?" Brian shouted to an empty apartment.

He didn't remember much about the film other than the chap responsible for *[Rec],* Jaume Balagueró, had directed it, and it featured a creepy apartment caretaker who'd developed an obsession with one of his tenants. He'd liked watching her. He'd enjoyed peeping. The caretaker was far removed from Brian. Brian wasn't the type of bloke to peep. To prove the point, he wrote a note on a yellow Post-it and affixed it to the fridge so he could address things in the morning: "Call estate agents about hole." He poured a large measure of bourbon, put on some Roger Waters, and resumed unpacking. And he did not peep.

THREE

THE FOLLOWING DAY Brian made decent progress transforming his apartment from house to home. When he heard the noise, he was pacing the living room, admiring his hard work, and humming along to Blood Ceremony. DVDs and CDs in racks, framed Pink Floyd *Dark Side of the Moon* print hanging in the centre of the living room, incense sticks burning. Truth be told, he felt it before he heard it. The floor started to tremor and Brian wondered if he was experiencing a minor earthquake. There'd been one around a decade ago, down in Kent, when he was an undergrad, so it was possible. He paused the music, cutting short Alia O'Brien's flute-work.

The sound came from next door. Brian went into the hall where he could hear better. If yesterday was the pre-show, then this right here was the main event. Slow rhythmic drumming, monk-like humming, and female vocals singing in a language he didn't understand. It sounded as if the drumming and monks were a backing track, but the female voice definitely emanated from the adjacent apartment. Some weird party, perhaps?

His interest piqued, Brian opened the wardrobe and removed the top towel from the heap on the shelf and peeped through the hole.

At first, he didn't understand. His brain refusing to register what was happening next door. The room was dark, save for two large candles—red wax and black pillar holders—resting on a chest of drawers at the far side of the room. In the foreground was the woman from the car park—Yoga Pants—her body gyrating to the beat of the music as she began to scream what sounded like an incantation. She wasn't wearing her yoga pants, wasn't wearing a thing. The candlelight did little to illuminate her features, but none of that mattered. He could see she was in great shape, slim yet muscular. Her skin lit up red, movements too erratic to be alluring, and still . . . Brian definitely felt *something*—transfixed as he watched her dance, heard her song, admired the swell of her form and the precision of her movements. He didn't know who she was or what she was doing, but he found himself unable to look away.

Each time Yoga Pants' hands moved to the swell of her breasts, Brian swelled too. When Yoga Pants swayed her hips, Brian also swayed. And when she looked directly into the hole, right at him—like it was meant to be—and sang such sweet liquor, only for him, Brian had to clasp his hands over his mouth to keep from screaming.

As she danced and pulsated and teased him, Brian caught his hands creeping towards his jeans. He moved them away, embarrassed at their outburst, scalding them for attempting to sabotage and sully this special moment. When he caught them creeping again, he stormed off and reprimanded them in the kitchen.

THEY'RE WATCHING

The next night it happened again, and the night after that, *and* the night after that. Same song, same time, same wild yet utterly mesmerising dance. Initially, Brian had felt ashamed, like he was no better than that piece-of-shit caretaker in the Balagueró film, but a few days in, shame turned to excitement and Brian began to look forward to her nightly cavorting. He couldn't help himself. Straining to see, he'd watch until his vision blurred, trying to make out the details of her face and body. Anything to satiate his appetite for her. Other than her lithe limbs and the small patch of hair between her legs, there were no features he could detect in the dim candlelight.

She was intoxicating, she *delighted* him, and she formed an important part of his evening ritual: a couple of whiskeys and some Netflix, followed by the headliner, *Her. Her* was a better fit than the previous moniker, *Yoga Pants*—ugh, so crude, so debasing, so utterly unworthy of *Her*.

Her was majestic.

Her was energy.

Her was *everything*.

There was no gym bro neighbour, no man next door, no boyfriend, just *Her*. Brian knew because he'd paid special attention to the movements in and out of the apartment. Brian didn't like to think of it as an obsession, more admiration. And make no mistake, *Her* was complicit. As Brian watched through that little gateway to heaven, *Her* danced for him, *Her* sang for him, *Her* exhilarated him.

FOUR

BRIAN WAS IN high spirits, Sunday morning, as he spoke with Helen over Skype and made coffee. The fresh smell of the ocean breeze carried through the open window.

"Well, there's this beautiful woman next door . . . " Brian pursed his lips to keep from laughing. *And she dances naked to this weird song almost every night.*

"Ask her out," Helen said whilst trying to feed Gracie. Each time Helen brought the spoon closer to Gracie's mouth, she'd turn her head. Helen was patient, waited until Gracie looked at the image on the laptop, then slipped the pureed food in. Gracie grimaced and spat the food onto her bib. "*Gracie*, darling, you've got to eat."

"What are you feeding her?"

"Peas. She normally likes them, but lately she's been finicky. Anyway, have you asked your neighbour out yet or what?"

Brian turned the volume down on his laptop. He didn't want *Her* to hear. "I've barely even seen her. She's pretty. Works out a lot too."

"A bodybuilder, then? Sure hope she's not on steroids. Ugh, the acne they get, I've seen pictures. You certainly don't want a woman with larger muscles than you."

"No, not a bodybuilder. I think she's a dancer."

"Ooh, ballet?"

"No, no, nothing like that. I don't know . . . "

"This is *why* you need to talk to her. She'd probably like the company."

Brian shook his head. "I'm not very good at introducing myself like that."

Gracie squealed at the camera, delighting in the Skype image. Helen shovelled another spoonful of green mush into her mouth. This time, Gracie accepted the spoon, holding down the peas. "She's not going to do all the work for you. Women still like to be approached, as long as you're not a creep about it."

Thanks for reminding me. "I'll think of something I need to borrow . . . I dunno, maybe some milk or eggs?"

"Hmm, not exactly original, but at least it'll give you a chance to talk to her."

"Well, it's a lot better than just knocking on her door. 'Hello, I'm Brian, would you like to go out?'"

"I didn't mean like that, silly." Helen sniggered. "Matter of fact, anything that involves you knocking on doors is best avoided. Remember that Valentine's Day you did knock-a-door run at Georgina Crawford's house and they called the bomb squad?"

Brian reddened. "I was twelve years old! And how was I supposed to know her father had been getting death threats?"

"Who leaves a brown cardboard box at someone's front door as a Valentine's gift? No bow or ribbon, no flowers."

"I'd spent all my pocket money on the chocolates inside the box!"

"You didn't even draw a heart."

Gracie tried to pull the spoon from Helen's hand. "Gracie, no." Without warning, his niece erupted into tears, wailing long and loud.

"Well, you've done it now." Brian scratched his beard. What if *Her* wasn't into beards?

Helen frowned. "Oh dear, sounds like somebody's ready for a nap. Oh, hey, when do you start your job?"

"Orientation's in four weeks."

"Why such a wait?"

Brian sipped his coffee, now lukewarm. "Well, it's kind of complicated and I don't want to bore you with the details, but with the new and old jobs being in different locations and departments, they have separate operating structures. Truth be told, the parent company's about the only thing they *do* have in common. I actually had to resign from the old position. Normally it's two weeks' notice, but cos I was relocating, they said I didn't have to work my notice. Advised against it, in fact. Said it'd give me a chance to settle into the new area."

Gracie was sniffling, resting her head on Helen's shoulder. "Such a shame you're all alone out there. You know you can visit anytime. Might do you some good to get out of the apartment."

Brian smiled. "Thanks, but I've got plenty to keep me occupied here."

"Well then, get over your shyness and talk to the girl next door. You've got nothing to lose."

"I'll try."

Helen looked stern, narrowing her eyes. "There is no try, only do."

"All right. Yoda you are not."

THEY'RE WATCHING

They laughed and said their goodbyes.

Brian reached for the remote and opened Netflix, knowing he'd spend almost as much time looking for something to watch as he would have spent watching if he'd picked something at random and pressed play straight away. But that was part of the allure, part of the times: Instagram, Snapchat, reality television, the want-it-now generation. Always looking for something better, never content.

We have everything at our fingertips, yet we're all so lonely. Brian shuddered at the thought. Considered Helen's parting advice. She was right, of course. When it came to women, the shyness that had crippled Brian when he was younger had only thickened with age. The strange thing was that most of his relationships were long. He'd dated Cynthia for three years and had genuinely believed he'd marry her. They were friends now, but when he'd suspected her of cheating, she hadn't denied it. The most hurtful part, she'd been with another man for almost a year right under his nose. He'd believed her lies, and she'd broken his heart. Cheating was a symptom, not the cause of a broken relationship, he understood that now and harboured no ill will towards Cynthia.

Brian's problem wasn't just shyness. It was an unwillingness to open up to women. To have conversations with depth. He'd freeze, hands clammy, and start stuttering as if he was back in high school. Since Cynthia there'd been nothing but easy women looking for a good time. And he'd been an easy man. Quick moments of electric passion, brief glimpses of happiness and what could be. Helen would have said his standards were too high, that he was looking for perfection. The truth was, he didn't know what he was looking for, doubted he'd know if it bumped right into him.

❧

Brian was about to head to bed when he heard the music coming from next door.

Right on time.

He turned out all the lights and went to the wardrobe. Pushing the towels aside and detaching the bar. He closed the wardrobe, making it as dark as possible. Trapping himself in with *Her*. If he leant his shoulder against the wall, he could peer through the gap without pulling any muscles in his neck. Candlelight flickered through the opening.

Strange that she had never noticed the hole in her own apartment. Yet, sometimes he swore she could see him watching her, that she enjoyed it, but that was part of the fantasy. Or was it?

When he looked into her room, there was no one there. Brian's heart beat faster, panicked. The candles were lit, but this time there was also a small lamp, illuminated in the corner, affording him a better view of the room. He was looking into her bedroom.

Her bedroom.

Her sanctuary.

He exhaled, taking it all in—a bed in the corner, a small nightstand to the left, next to it a wardrobe against the wall. Boxes lay on the floor, beside the wardrobe. *She hasn't even finished unpacking.* Movement to the left caught Brian's eye and he watched *Her* enter the room, wearing a silk robe. It looked like a kimono, only shorter, and completely black with no designs or embroidering.

She turned to the side, and for the first time, Brian saw her face. The light wasn't strong enough to make out much detail, but from what he could see, she appeared to be of Asian descent. She picked up a small remote from the edge of the bed and suddenly the music was much louder. Trance-like rhythm, almost tribal. Turning to face him, staring straight ahead as though looking into his eyes, she untied the robe and let it fall to the floor. The candlelight flickered shadows across her body like tongues, licking and teasing her.

Her.

Brian watched, but he did not touch.

FIVE

BRIAN HAD ONLY slept in the apartment six nights and was already getting jittery. He lived near the coast but had yet to make it out to the seafront. He went on a walk around the local area to see what he could discover. He never found the seafront and wound up in the town centre, via some roundabout way. Still, he stumbled upon an independent coffee shop with a lot of character. You could tell they were big on health from the kale chips, organic single-origin coffee, and gluten-free treats. Cute barista, too, with a nose ring and pink hair which seemed pretty out-there for what was otherwise a small conservative town. But Brian wasn't interested in the girl with pink hair—'Lexie' according to her nametag. She was a little on the young side, and besides he felt attached to *Her*. They'd shared something together. For Brian to flirt with others would be a betrayal of sorts. What he *was* interested in were the two bookcases stacked full of second-hand books. Yellowed pages, wonderfully musty scents perfumed with the passing of time, cracked spines, and worn pages. Best of all, the chalkboard sign overhead read, 'Customers read for free. Grab a book.'

THEY'RE WATCHING

Does that mean non-customers can read for a fee?

Brian bought an americano and a gluten-free chocolate brownie, then set up shop at a table in the far-corner, before heading back to the bookcases. Memories of childhood: Herbert, King, Rice, Bradbury, Jackson, Masterton. Brian was spoilt for choice. In the end, he picked up Stephen King's *Night Shift*. He'd only read King's novels and figured short stories were the perfect form for kicking back for a few hours in a coffee house.

When Brian heard the commotion, he was nearing the end of 'Graveyard Shift'. Hall and Warwick had just discovered the surprise in the basement. Lord knows how long the raucous outside had been going on for, but it sounded like a bunch of lads celebrating a big win at the footie—hollering and cheering, chanting and clapping. He set the book down. After a quick stretch of his arms to ease some back pain, Brian strolled over to the window. It was the man with the long-flowing robe. He walked down the street, shaking hands with residents and exchanging greetings. Same as he'd done in the supermarket. People were treating him like a celebrity. Back in the Midlands, someone dressed up like that would be lucky to get a nod of the head, let alone a 'hello'. Amongst the commotion, a tank-like bloke wearing a Hobgoblin t-shirt screamed, "We love you!" prompting half the crowd to fall to their knees in a bow before getting up as if nothing out of the ordinary had happened.

"What's his story?" Brian looked towards Lexie, her head downcast, probably on her phone, though he couldn't say for sure, the countertop obscuring his view.

She said nothing. Didn't even move.

"Who is he?" A little louder.

This time Lexie looked up, forced a smile. "More coffee?"

"Erm . . . yeah . . . sure." Brian had expected an answer, not another question, and then the social anxiety kicked in, the words tangling in his mouth.

He took the fresh coffee and retreated to his table, opening the book once more, but he was out of the story. Unable to focus.

Who the hell is Red Robe?

SIX

BACK AT HIS APARTMENT, Brian battered a fish fillet and sliced a potato thick for chips. Like most of his best kitchenware, Helen had bought him the deep fat fryer as a birthday gift. He considered making a salad but had forgotten to pick up cherry tomatoes at the supermarket.

"What's this? You bring me a salad with no cherry tomatoes . . . I don't want it, take it back," Brian said in the worst Pacino impression ever. Unable to remember who said the quote, or if it even existed, he settled into cooking.

After dinner he was stuffed and sleepy. He'd eaten so much fat, he could practically feel his arteries suffocating. The sun was about to set. Red and golden rays peered through the blinds, illuminating swirls of dust motes in the air.

Brian poured a bourbon and flopped onto the sofa. It was time to begin his evening ritual. He rubbed his hands together in glee, then fired up Netflix. A few times he found himself closing his eyes, but whenever he let them stay shut, sleep refused to come. He was turning into an insomniac. Too alive with anticipation for *Her*, then too hyped-up to settle afterwards. He hoped things would change once he started working.

Whilst deciding between *Black Mirror* and *The OA*, Brian heard raised voices from outside the apartment. He peered through the blinds outside but saw nothing other than his and his neighbour's car. There wasn't anyone or anything else in the car park. Someone was shouting, though, no doubt about it. He held his breath and listened hard. He heard a woman talking loudly but couldn't make out the words. Maybe it was *Her*, watching TV.

In the hall, the sound grew louder. It wasn't the TV. It was *Her*. She was talking to someone. Hers was the only voice. She had to be on the phone.

Brian hurried to the wardrobe and pulled the towels aside, tossing the hanging bar to the floor. All the lights were on in her room. He could see *Her*, wearing jeans and a t-shirt, pacing barefoot on the carpet. She was talking—no, *yelling*—into the phone. But it wasn't English, which was why he couldn't understand her. He concentrated hard. Ear rather than eye pressed against the hole. *Japanese!* He'd seen enough Takashi Miike and Hideo Nakata films to distinguish Japanese from other East Asian languages. Whatever the conversation was about, she was angry. Hell, she was *furious*. She paced, listening to whoever was on the other line. Was this her boyfriend? Maybe her ex-boyfriend? Was she going through a nasty divorce? A custody battle, perhaps?

She let loose a flurry of words, none of them understandable until the last few which were most certainly English, " . . . quit being a dick and fucking figure it out." Her accent was English, but he couldn't place the region. Eye back against the peephole, he watched as she flung the phone onto the bed, then ran her hands through her hair. Even whilst performing mundane actions she exuded elegance. A grace despite her obvious frustration. After a couple of deep breaths, she walked out of Brian's view. He continued to gaze, feasting his hungry eyes upon where she'd been. Straining to hear. After a few minutes, she returned and picked up the remote next to her phone on the bed. Pounding drums thumped through the speakers, music far removed from her night-time dancing numbers. As Rob Zombie chanted about his 'Dragula', she pulled her t-shirt off and began to dance. Brian couldn't take his eyes off her. She kicked her jeans, then her lacy black knickers, to the floor, and gyrated in front of him with wild abandon. He'd never seen her dance this way before. Her dancing was never conventional, it always had a volatile edge, but coupled with its erraticism was a flow, a smoothness, a grace—what Brian thought of as interpretative dance. But this . . . this was sexy, raunchy even. She ran her hands over her breasts, spending a little time at her nipples, gripping and twisting them. Standing straight, she arched her back and grabbed her arse, squeezing her buttocks so hard Brian could see her hands' prints. For a second, she leant forward and bounced. Twerking. Her hands went between her legs and she turned her head so Brian could see the side of her face.

Turned on, he unbuckled his trousers and let them fall to his ankles. He loved this new side to *Her*, and there was no turning back. For either of them. He barely touched himself, almost came right there and then. He took a few measured breaths before continuing. Brian grabbed himself once more, easing up-and-down. Up-and-down. Eyes fixed. Never leaving her body.

She was still touching herself, her motions growing more frantic. Her eyes closed, fingers disappearing into *Her*, musk filling the air.

A loud tone sounded off behind Brian, pulling him back to reality. *What the . . . ?* He smacked his head against the wall.

Oh shit!

The tone continued. He stopped masturbating, realising it was Helen on Skype. He'd forgotten to turn the volume down on his laptop, and the sound was blaring through his speakers. Was it loud enough for *Her* to hear, too? She'd probably heard his head thunk the wall, the oaf that he was. Had he blown it? Exposed himself as a peeper? Brian looked through the gap, fearing the worst.

Relieved, he saw she was still on her knees, still touching herself, still lost to all but the pleasure.

Skype continued to sing.

Damn it, Helen. Your timing is the fucking worst.

He shoved his still erect penis into his trousers, tucking it into the waistband, and went into the living room to see what all the fuss from Helen was about, hoping his face didn't look too flushed.

Brian answered in time, breathing heavily.

"What is it?" It came out colder than intended.

"Hey Brian. Hope I haven't caught you at a bad time."

"It's a little late, but it's okay, I wasn't up to much." *Just wanking over my neighbour, we do things differently down here.*

"Great. Gracie just—have you been exercising?"

"Um, no." Brian wiped sweat from his forehead as if hiding the evidence.

"Anyway, as I was saying, Gracie just got to sleep, so I thought we could have a proper catch-up. Last time you were ever so busy, what with unpacking and everything."

Brian reached for the glass of bourbon, still half-full, took a swig.

"So, tell me, have there been any developments with that girl?" Her eyes lit-up, hungry for gossip, something juicy.

"It's been little over twenty-four hours, give me a chance, I'm working up to it." *I'm working up something.*

"You seem distracted."

He *was* distracted. How could he not be distracted? Cock-blocked by his own sister.

"You're right, I am distracted." There was no point lying about that at least, he just had to come up with a reason. Something. Anything. "It's this apartment, nothing major, guess I'm being silly, but god damn it they advertised the place as 'like new' and it isn't. Only small things, but things I've got to fix, like holes in the wall."

"Holes in the wall?"

"Yeah. Not very big holes, mind, but filling them in is one more thing to add to my ever-increasing to-do list. I'm stressed thinking about the new job, too."

Helen was quiet. Brian thought about everything his sister had to do and realised how pathetic he must sound, moaning about a bit of DIY. He was making himself out to be such a loser, but he'd had to think fast. *And that was the best I could come up with? Holes in the wall? The fuck is wrong with me?*

"So, there's this guy I know, Phil, who runs a home improvements business in Solihull. Keith introduced us when I needed the kitchen doing. Obviously he's not going to travel all the way down to you, but he has connections. I'll bet I can swing something so he can put you in touch with someone who can take care of things."

"No! I mean, *no thank you*. I appreciate it, but it sounds like a lot of money. I can nip into town—they probably have a Wilko or someplace I can buy filler and do it on the cheap."

"If money's the problem, you know I can help."

"I know, I know. And thanks, Helen. Seriously. Like I said, I *really* do appreciate it. Anyway, listen to me, whining about bloody holes in the wall, when you have a full-time job and kid to take care of. Truth is, I've had too much whiskey and too little sleep. But I know you didn't call this late just to have a catch-up, what's going on?"

"If you're tired, you should sleep. How about I call you sometime tomorrow?"

Brian could tell from her voice and the way she'd avoided his question that something was up. He let the silence linger, knowing Helen wouldn't stand it for long, would be forced to fill it.

"So, there was *something*. I might go to Germany soon—not permanently—but for a couple of days in the next month or so, and if that goes well . . . " Her arm reached off-camera, returning with a small glass of white wine which she sipped. "Well, we'll cross that bridge when we come to it."

That threw Brian. Helen had seemed upset about him moving three hours away and now she was talking about what exactly? Living in Germany?

THEY'RE WATCHING

"Don't worry, I won't be *living* there or anything." It was as if the question was stitched to his face. Helen had always been intuitive. "There's no way that would work, especially not with Gracie being so young—and Keith would be devastated, I can't do that to him after all he's done for us—but it *is possible* there'll be more trips in the future. Anyway, no point either of us worrying about that now. Like I said, we'll talk about it when the time's right." She drank another mouthful of wine. "Well then, I'll call you on my lunch break tomorrow, how's that?"

Brian told her it sounded great. They said their goodbyes and ended the call. For a few seconds he stared at the screen wondering what the hell was going on, what the Germany trip meant for him, for her, for Gracie. Helen hadn't come out and said it, but Brian reckoned she'd want him to look after Gracie at least some of the time. She felt bad enough relying on Keith as much as she did, but to ask him to do even more? Helen was a proud woman, she wouldn't trouble Keith, which meant the care would fall to Brian. He wasn't ready for that—he could barely take care of himself.

Brian's concern was quick to evaporate when he remembered *Her* and what she'd been in the middle of.

What *they'd* been in the middle of.

Brian practically ran to the peephole in anticipation.

But the room was empty.

The show now over.

SEVEN

THE NEXT MORNING Brian drove to an out-of-town retail park with a Wilko, Halfords, Next, Currys, and the big Sainsbury's he'd seen on Google Maps when he first moved in. He'd had to drive past the level crossing to get there, but unlike the first time, hadn't had to wait five minutes for a train to pass through.

Inside Wilko, Brian grabbed a couple of runner mats to protect the kitchen floor and tossed them into the trolley, along with a couple of potted snake plants.

He couldn't stop thinking about *Her*.

"That's forty-eight pounds, mate," the bloke at the checkout said. From the tone of his voice, Brian guessed it wasn't the first time either. Brian snapped to attention and retrieved his Visa card. Taking his receipt, he headed outside where he froze.

A young woman wearing baggy cargo trousers and a t-shirt was loading bags into her car boot. Her hair was pulled back in a ponytail and she had those wide sunglasses on again. There was no doubt in Brian's mind.

It was *Her*.

His mouth went dry.

He watched her slam the boot shut, then push her trolley to the return bay.

THEY'RE WATCHING

It was now or never.

But what the hell am I supposed to say to Her?

She was getting closer to her car, keys in hand.

Brian took a deep breath and pushed his trolley towards the parking area. His car was only a few down from hers, so this would look natural. Whatever *this* was. He really didn't know what he was going to say. His insides quivering.

She was about to open her car door when he called out to her. "Hello, neighbour!"

Her hand dropped. She turned to look at him, somewhat defensively.

Brian held up his hands. "Sorry, thought you were someone else."

She looked at him, raising her sunglasses. Recognition crossed her face. "Hey, wait, you *are* my new neighbour, aren't you?"

Brian smiled. "I thought for a second you might not have been the right neighbour. I mean . . . well, I wouldn't have any other neighbours here now, would I?" He stood up straight, trying to appear less awkward than he sounded, and held his hand out to *Her.* "I'm sorry. My name's Brian."

She took his hand in hers. "Nice to finally meet you, Brian. The estate agents told me I'd have a neighbour soon. I'm Yuki."

"Yuki . . . Japanese, right?"

"On my mother's side."

"Never been to Japan, but it's on my bucket list."

Yuki laughed. Her smile was genuine. "I've only been a few times myself, can't wait to go back."

"Flights must be expensive."

She nodded and Brian realised it had been a dumb thing to say, too obvious. "I remembered you from the first day I arrived at Pelagic Court—recognised you instantly."

"Hmm, didn't realise I made such an impression."

You have no idea. Brian cleared his throat. "Live there all by yourself?"

"Yes, but it's only temporary, I'm afraid."

"Oh, you have to break your lease?"

She shook her head. "Oh no, nothing like that. I just meant it's not where I'd like to spend the rest of my life."

Brian remembered the note through the door, 'Get Out'. Was there something more sinister going on here? He went to ask but realised however he said it he'd wind up sounding creepy, the words betraying his intentions.

The sun was bearing down on Brian—a drop of sweat dribbled down his back. Moisture streaked over Yuki's forehead and down past her eyes. "Well, it's getting warm, huh?" Brian said.

She wiped her brow with the back of her hand. She wasn't saying anything. Was she waiting for him to ask her out? He couldn't read her, couldn't be sure. He took the plunge. "Say, how would you like to go for a drink sometime?"

Her eyes lit up. "Coffee okay?"

"Is it okay? I bloody love the stuff, you could hook me up to an IV drip of coffee and I still wouldn't have enough." *Hook me up to an IV? In what situation would I possibly want that? I need to stop talking. Deep breaths, Brian. Deep breaths.*

"Me, too. That sounds like a wonderful idea." She dug into her handbag and retrieved a pen. She found a piece of chewing gum, unwrapped it, put it in her mouth, then wrote her number on the paper.

Brian took the paper. "Well, I could have knocked on your door." He grinned.

"Uh, yeah, I almost forgot."

"But I will call you. And soon."

She took Brian's hand again. Her touch was soft. "Yes, please. Let's do this."

When he was back in the car and certain she was out of sight, he fist-punched the air and let out a howl of joy. *Sounds like a wonderful idea . . . let's do this.* He replayed her words all the way home.

Back at the apartment, Brian set the snake plants on either side of the apartment's front door and laid out the runners in the kitchen. He was starving, so made a sandwich, piling thin slices of smoked ham and spicy turkey on thick cut wholemeal bread. After putting his dishes in the dishwasher, he turned on the TV and searched for something to watch. Yuki's number was still in his pocket, burning a hole. Now that he finally had something to say, he wanted to Skype Helen and tell her about his progress but decided to wait until after the date.

This was the first time Brian had asked someone out and got a "*yes*" straight away. And all he did was ask a simple, direct question.

It was stupid, really, to think fear had been holding him back for so long. For the first time in a long time, Brian felt more confident. It wasn't like he was going to have women falling over him anytime soon, but it was a much-needed boost.

He put on *Black Mirror.* Had heard good things about it but until now hadn't had the time to jump in. After the first episode, he was hooked. Three episodes deep, and it was dark outside.

She has to be home by now.

Brian lowered the volume, listening for *Her* next door.

Silence.

He couldn't resist. A few seconds later he was peeping at her bedroom through the gap. He was met with darkness. His own breathing, the only sound.

EIGHT

GETTING TO SLEEP was difficult that night. Brian hadn't seen *Her* dance and when he'd eventually settled in bed, he'd been unable to think about anything but *Her*. Though, of course, she wasn't called *Her*. Her name was Yuki. Yet to Brian she would always be *Her*. It was more sublime, more ethereal, more fitting.

It was more *Her*.

―◄▮►―

Brian got up with the sun. He'd just been lying there, dreaming about the coffee date, playing out different ways it could go—things he'd mess up, phrases that'd spill out wrong, apologies he'd have to make as way of clarification:

"I can't believe this is actually happening, in many ways I've been dreaming about this since I first saw you . . . I mean figuratively, I'm not *actually* dreaming about you, I'm not obsessed or anything . . . That came out wrong. I'm saying you're nice and I'm lucky to be dating you . . . not that we're dating but—"

Fuck! Brian didn't know what to say to women. He barely knew what to say to men. The more he thought about it, the more he wondered how he'd been with

Cynthia for so long. *Because you were a bloody doormat, mate. You let her walk all over you.* Nah, that wasn't quite right. He'd let a few things slide and true, it had been her infidelity that had officially finished things, but you didn't end a beautiful relationship because of one mistake, not if you had any sense. Humans err, it's what we're prone to do, and Brian and Cynthia had erred multiple times for months. *Doormat* . . . that was some bullshit the twats at work had come out with because he refused to treat his partners like dirt. The HR Manager, Gary Holden, had been the worst: "treat 'em mean, keep 'em keen, mate." Brian had seen the bruises on Gary's wife and he wasn't interested in his 'life advice'. Only thing Gary was good at was being a cunt.

Brian went on this way for much of the morning, thinking about *Her* and past relationships, about moulding his future into something better than days past. He tried watching more *Black Mirror,* then tried reading some fiction online, but couldn't get into anything—his mind abuzz. Truth be told, he wanted to ring *Her* there and then and ask if she was up for that coffee. But he couldn't be too eager. Didn't want to appear desperate or creepy.

You're a peeper, you are *creepy, embrace it.*

He wouldn't embrace it. Matter of fact, maybe he'd drive back to Wilko and buy some filler for that hole in the wall, start making some changes for the better. If she ever found out about what he'd done he could kiss goodbye to a friendly relationship with her, let alone a romantic one.

➳〳∖➳

THEY'RE WATCHING

In the end Brian didn't drive to Wilko, but he didn't look through the hole either, so he was taking small steps in the right direction. *If you feel proud for not perving on someone for a couple of hours, you should probably kill yourself.* Brian brushed the thought aside. *Whatever.* He was doing well.

He'd call Yuki at seven. Any earlier would be too soon, any later and it might disrupt her evening. Hell, if he got lucky maybe she'd demand they go immediately. *Yeah, that will never happen.*

Mid-afternoon the apartment doorbell rang. He looked through the peephole expecting to see cold callers peddling religion or cleaning services.

But he saw *Her.*

He didn't answer straight away. Instead, rushing to the bathroom to check his hair was all right and applying a splash of cologne. He didn't have much hair but thought it was diligent to ensure the few hairs he had were in place. Once he was satisfied he looked good, or more accurately that he was the right side of average, he opened the door.

"Oh, Yuki!" he said, keeping his cool. "What a wonderful surprise."

"Hey, Brian."

God, he liked the sound of his name in her mouth.

She was wearing denim short shorts with a black off-the-shoulder top. The splashes of bare skin were almost too much for Brian to handle. "You didn't call," she said, pouting.

Shit, I've messed this up before it's even begun— played the long game like a dickhead when I should have phoned her. Why didn't I call?

She started laughing. Even her giggles sounded divine. "I'm just playing with you. It's hardly been twenty-four hours."

"Exactly!" Brian laughed, too, but it was forced and sounded like a donkey being kicked in the stomach mid-whinny. "Who would call after twenty-four hours . . . *laaaame*?" Yuki wasn't laughing with him. "I mean, I suppose some people *would* call, but . . . " He slapped the doorframe, louder than intended, was going for playful but sounded angry. "I'm *messing* with you, too . . . got you!"

She didn't react. Her eyes glanced to the plants. "Well that certainly gives the place a bit of character."

"Right?" Brian said. "And snake plants also remove all sorts of nastiness from the air. So if there's any bad juju around here, I've got us covered."

"Bad *juju*?"

Crap, Brian couldn't decide whether her smile was jolly or disgusted.

Yuki bent down and touched one of the plants. "Is this even real?"

"Um, I sure hope so."

"And where'd you get it?"

"Wilko."

Yuki giggled. God damn it, was the plant a fake? And he was what? A *laughing stock*?

"A man can buy a faux plant if he wants," Brian shouted.

Yuki bit down on her lip. "So, anyway, I was thinking, if you're free, we could get that coffee now."

"Now . . . "

"I know it's awfully sudden, so if you're busy working we can schedule—"

THEY'RE WATCHING

"Working? I don't even have a job . . . Christ, that came out a little off, I mean I *have* a job but it doesn't start for a while, and of course there are things to do around the apartment . . . but *bloody hell* why not get a coffee, eh? If we don't get a coffee then what's the point of coffee houses even existing?"

"For other people to get coffee?"

"Yeah, but . . . look, give me a few and we'll get this show on the road."

They agreed to meet outside in five minutes. Brian closed the door and started whistling as he got ready for the big coffee date. He replayed the conversation in his head—he'd have to get better at this, and fast.

———※———

Yuki drove, which Brian didn't mind, but it felt a bit strange. He expected to be chauffeuring *Her*, not the other way around.

"So, what kind of work do you do?" he asked.

"Right now, I'm an unemployed dance instructor."

"Dance? Like ballet?"

"Some, but not as much as I'd like. My sauté is a little weak."

"Saw *Tay*? Isn't that cooking?"

Yuki giggled. "It's one way to get *en pointe*. You know, on the tips of your toes?"

"Oh yes. That looks . . . difficult."

"It's a bitch. I prefer just dancing, or what you might call interpretative. Though I can do a mean foxtrot."

"The only dance move I know is 'shaking my arse'. I mean, not *my* arse, I'm not really built for that, but you know what I mean . . . "

49

Yuki turned the vehicle into the car park. They were in an area of the town Brian hadn't explored yet. "Hmm, I don't think I've ever heard of that style . . . Shaking my *arse*." Brian wasn't sure if he'd imagined the emphasis or if it was where his head was at. "You don't mean 'twerking', do you?"

Brian laughed.

"Hey, don't knock it. I've taught twerking, and it's a damn fine workout."

"You mean people actually take lessons to learn how to twerk?"

"Build it, and they will come. Speaking of which, we're here."

Yuki parked, grabbed her small handbag, and stood waiting for Brian to get out of the car, before tapping the remote to lock up. "Here it is, the best coffee house in the world."

Brian looked at the building, trying to find a name, or some distinguishing mark. There was nothing. "What's this place called?"

"It doesn't really have a name, which is why it's so special." She held out her arm. "Let's go inside and grab a table."

Brian hooked his arm in hers and they walked in together. Here he was, just some average Joe with the most beautiful woman in the world at his side. Brian imagined all the customers were staring at them in awe. Look at *Her*, so powerful, so exquisite, so otherworldly. And for a brief second, everyone's eyes *were* upon them. But once they realised there wasn't anything special about the two of them, they went back about their business, drinking lattes and eating sandwiches.

But we are special.

The sun was peeking through the clouds, so they found a table on the back patio outside, before returning inside to order their coffees. "So, how'd you find this place?" Brian asked.

"When I first moved in, the movers took their time getting my stuff to me, so I went exploring. I'm not a big fan of the franchise coffee shops. As soon as I saw this place, I knew it was exactly what I was looking for. It's difficult to explain but sometimes you just feel an instant connection, you know?"

Brian nodded. He knew all right. Oh God, did he know. "There's another independent in town—"

"With the girl with the pink hair, you mean?"

"Right."

"Ugh, no way, customer service is non-existent in that place. Pinky's always on her phone and she even tried to overcharge me."

Brian didn't tell *Her* he thought Lexie was pleasant, or that he remembered her name, or that the used books were a nice touch.

"How long was it until the movers turned up with your things?"

"Three days, and I'll say, sleeping on the floor is not all it's cracked up to be, even if it is commonplace back in Japan."

"That's insane. Guess I was lucky—all my things arrived the day I moved in. It's a cool place, though I don't get why there are so many fish illustrations and sculptures."

"The fish are *definitely* weird. The estate agents said they're going to install the fixtures soon, but I haven't seen them yet."

"Fixtures?"

"For the fish torches."

Brian wrinkled his nose. "Torches? Hmm, and all this time I thought those fish were fountains."

The barista arrived with their coffees. Brian could get used to coffee shops with table service. He watched as Yuki poured a small amount of cream into her coffee, then added a sprinkle of vanilla, only to top it off with an obscene amount of sugar.

"I like sugar," she said, when she caught him staring. "Want to know how I keep the weight off?"

"I would never—"

"High metabolism. I'd wager I could eat you under the table."

"Oh, a challenge? I'm game."

"You'll lose. I could have been a competitive eater."

Brian poured some cream into his coffee. "I've never really understood all of that. Seems like an easy way to spend a lot of time in the toilet."

"Certainly. They train for the competitions, but it's not like you think."

Were they really going to talk about eating contests? "So, do you have any job prospects or interviews lined up?"

Yuki shook her head. "You sure you don't want to talk about how to eat sushi without chewing?" She laughed. "Okay, that's gross. And no, I don't, but I haven't been looking either. I was with the last studio for quite a while, and they had excellent benefits that gave me a little money when I left. But all good things come to an end, so I need to polish my CV and start the search."

"I don't know if I could do that."

"Do what? Be unemployed? Sometimes you have to take the risk. Things weren't going so well with the studio, so I left whilst the situation was tolerable. Truthfully, I was ready for a change. What kind of work do you do?"

"Medical Records. Well, more of a supervisory position." He didn't tell *Her* it was glorified data input, that he spent most days staring at Microsoft Excel, punctuated with the occasional telephone call, walks to the coffee machine, and shit-talking with colleagues. Maybe the new position would be different. That's what they'd promised—*more responsibility*, whatever that meant.

"You get to work from home?"

"I wish, but if that were the case I doubt I'd get much actual work done. Sadly, I have to work in a stuffy office, wear a tie, the whole damn mess."

"Keep in line, polish your shoes, play office politics. Now that kind of work is definitely not for me."

"What if they let you dance whilst you worked?"

Yuki laughed. "Now *that* would be different."

Now that *would be amazing*.

➤➤◆◆◆

They drank two more cups of coffee before Yuki announced it was time to head back. "I've got some friends I'm meeting up with later this evening."

"A hot date?"

"No, Brian, *you* are my hot date."

Brian blushed. "Well, thank you."

"No, thank *you*. This was fun. At least it was for me, and I hope it was for you, too."

"Yes, it was a lot of fun. I'll be honest with you, I'm . . . um . . . not very good at talking with women, but I can talk to you."

Yuki nodded. "I like that."

They drove back to the apartments, listening to the radio and making small talk. Brian walked *Her* to her door and lingered outside trying not to feel like a teenager. Yuki took his hands in hers and looked up at him. "I'm so glad you came with me today."

"Me too."

"Um, look . . . I'll save us both the trouble of being awkward here." She raised up on her tiptoes and kissed Brian on the corner of his mouth. "I like you. All you have to do is call me. Deal?"

"Deal."

Once he was inside, Brian rested against his door, heart hammering in his chest. She kissed him. He couldn't believe it. Sure, it wasn't a full-on passionate kiss, but it was a nice kiss, a caring kiss. He was a hundred percent positive he wasn't in the dreaded 'friend-zone'.

A kiss from *Her*.

It didn't seem real.

But it was.

༄

After watching Netflix for what seemed like hours, keeping the volume low so as not to miss her music playing next door, Brian switched the TV off and began getting ready for bed. Whilst brushing his teeth, he thought he heard *Her* returning home. He turned the tap off and listened. No, she wasn't home. Must have still been out with her friends. They'd come by earlier to go into town in their car.

Then he heard it again.

A sharp, quick sound, as though someone was snapping their fingers.

He spat out his toothpaste and wiped his hands, listening.

The sound came once more, only it wasn't coming from next door.

It was from the car park.

Brian walked into the bedroom and over to the window. Street light shone through the blind slats. He leant forward, adjusted the blinds to let more light in and get a better view.

There was a man in the car park.

He had longish hair and a full beard. Though the temperature was mild outside, he wore a thin knitted cardigan, buttoned all the way up to his neck, and dark jeans.

Brian was sure he'd never seen this man before.

The man stood near Yuki's car, staring up at her apartment. He bent down, his hands running over the concrete. He picked up a small pebble and tossed it at her window.

Was he her ex-boyfriend? She hadn't mentioned anyone earlier, but then he hadn't asked about anything like that.

Maybe he was a stalker.

Could he have been the man who'd posted the strange note through Brian's door? Brian stretched his hands through his thin hair, pulling at the roots. Fuck, what was he supposed to do? What was the *right thing* to do? Confront the man? Call the police? Brian felt his chest tightening and his throat go dry. He could go outside—he probably *should* go outside, to get a better reading on the situation. Brian grabbed an old glass of water from the windowsill and downed it to soothe his throat. He nearly spat it back out—it had gone stale and tepid. Brian looked back to the man who quickly turned and started walking away. Brian strained his eyes watching the man, but as soon as he was out of the car park, he disappeared into the night.

NINE

"I'M JUST SAYING, what kind of bloke throws stones at someone's window? Hasn't he got a mobile phone or something?" Brian gazed at Lexie, looking for answers.

They sat opposite one another in the otherwise empty coffee shop. Brian had gone into town to unwind—he'd felt especially stressed upon waking and not just because he'd forgotten to buy more eggs and coffee. It had been the man who'd done it, that and the fact he hadn't seen Yuki all morning. He should've texted her, but didn't want to seem clingy, so instead had gone for a stroll. The cool air against his neck and the scent of damp grass had helped. Though not enough, evidently. As soon as he'd entered the coffee shop, Lexie had asked if everything was all right with a look that told Brian it was more than politeness. The worry must have been etched across his face. Brian told Lexie about the man and his concerns whilst she nodded along.

"Am I being silly? Overthinking it?" Brian scratched his head. "Yuki lives there all by herself, seems like keeping an eye out for her is the decent thing to do. And there was something about the bloke . . . something not quite right, though I

57

couldn't place it. Well, anyway, I've taken up enough of your time."

"There are no customers here," Lexie said. "And I'm happy to listen. It's nice to find someone who wants to talk."

Brian blushed, then chastised himself for doing so in front of someone who was not *Her*.

"Besides, what else am I gonna do? There are only so many true crime podcasts I can listen to. I've already blasted through most of *True Crime Garage* and *My Favorite Murder* and I'm halfway through *The Campbell Files*." Lexie smiled. "So, keep talking."

"Guess I'm being overly dramatic. Thinking about the worst-case scenario when there's likely a perfectly innocent explanation."

Lexie put her hand on top of Brian's. She had the softest touch but to Brian it felt as if there was something more to it, something alive, not exactly electrical but a kind of charge, unfamiliar and energising. "You're not overthinking anything. I think it's sweet that you care so much."

Sweet . . . A compliment or condescension? Brian looked into Lexie's eyes, there was no malice or sarcasm. "We need more people like you here," she said. "You're one of the good guys—someone who's not afraid to go out of his way to help others."

Brian wasn't so sure about that and yet Helen said similar—would often tell Brian he put others before himself, but unlike Lexie she seemed to think it was a weakness not a strength.

"What do I do, Lexie?" He hadn't meant to call her by her name, it had just spilt out, and yet he sensed her warm to it. To *him*.

"We look after each other."

For a moment Brian thought she was talking about the two of them then soon came to his senses.

"This is a good town, full of good people," Lexie said. "But that doesn't mean that bad shit doesn't happen, you know what I'm saying?"

Brian nodded, though wondered if he was missing some wider point. The way Lexie had put it she'd described most places he'd lived. "Is there much crime here?"

Lexie removed her hand from atop his, he instantly felt as if something were missing.

They remained in silence. Brian soon filled the gap. "It could explain the strange man in the car park, is all. Burglary, car theft, things like that . . . "

Lexie grinned, then put her hand to her mouth, stifling laugher. "That wasn't the kind of thing I was talking about."

"But it does ha—"

"Of course, it happens!" Tears of laughter streamed down Lexie's face and this time Brian felt the joke really was on him. Lexie wiped her face with the back of her hand and exhaled. "Brian, you're so . . . " But instead of words she beamed.

Lexie might have been in good spirits, but Brian swore this was the last time he filled an awkward silence. If he'd turned pink at her words earlier, now he was positively vermillion.

Lexie stalled, assessing Brian—her expression turned serious—before deciding it was okay to continue. "Something happened, a few years back . . . "

"Go on."

"I don't know if I should, I mean—fuck—this is dark *dark* stuff and we've only just met." Lexie ruffled her hair. "And yet I trust you, I really do. Is that naïve of me?"

Brian didn't know how to answer that and luckily he didn't have to as she soon continued. "It's an unsolved case—there's a person of interest we never tracked down."

"We?"

"Sorry, bad habit, it's just, the whole town takes what happened very personally."

"What did—"

"This man you saw—the prick throwing stones—was there anything *distinctive* about him?"

"It was pretty dark and the bloke seemed fairly nondescript. Long hair and beard, black or dark brown, but it was dark so even that might not be accurate."

"What about his build?"

"He was wearing some kind of jumper or cardigan . . . I mean, he wasn't fat, but he wasn't particularly gaunt either, so I guess average, but then again in the dark and without short sleeves you can't really tell, can you? Might have been he worked out." Brian sighed. "Sorry for being so useless."

A woman with shoulder length hair, a denim jacket, and vinyl leggings practically painted on entered the café with a short squat man in a beige t-shirt and corduroy trousers. The woman waited at the counter whilst the man settled at a window seat.

Lexie smiled at her, then leant across the table towards Brian, voice low. "Did this bloke have any tattoos, scars, piercings, anything like that?"

"Not that I remember. But that doesn't mean there weren't." *I should have taken a photo, why didn't I? Christ . . .* "This *case,* what exactly—"

"I really should get back to work," Lexie said, standing up and looking over at the woman. "But this conversation isn't over. I'll tell you more soon."

Brian stood and Lexie took his hand once more, as if to shake it—only instead of shaking it she simply held it, and Brian felt another surge of energy fill him up. By the time the rush had normalised Lexie was back behind the counter and serving the lady.

Brian headed towards the door, glancing over at the lady, but there was something about the way she silently regarded him that left Brian uneasy.

"I'll see you later, Brian," Lexie said.

He rushed out of the coffee shop, more confused than ever.

TEN

HELEN SIPPED HER tea, unable to hide the smile on her face. "So, you *actually* went on a date?"

"It was just coffee."

"But she knocked on your door, she took you up on the offer. This is good." She took another sip. "And yes, it was a date."

"I don't know about—"

"A date, and I'll not hear you call it anything else," she said, then chuckled. "Oh, Brian, I'm so proud of you."

Brian blushed. "It's nothing, really."

"Of course it is. Tell me all about it."

Brian recounted their date, trying to make it sound nonchalant. Yet, he couldn't help but feel somewhat confident about how he'd gone about the whole thing. Helen was always telling him he needed to grow a pair, and now that he had, he felt good. No way was he going to let her know that all her chiding had finally rubbed off on him.

"And all of this from seeing her out and about? Wonderful, just wonderful. Tell me, when is the next date?"

"I don't know. I kissed her and told her I'd call."

Helen clapped her hands together. "You kissed her?"

"Not full on the mouth. Right on the corner. But it counted."

"You must call her back. You see? She's interested in you. This is fantastic."

"I will call her, but not tonight."

Helen frowned. "I would."

"Wouldn't I sound too eager?"

"Maybe, but then she didn't waste any time knocking on your door, did she?"

"Well, perhaps I'll call her and thank her for the lovely time, make small talk."

"And find out when you can meet her again."

The whole thing seemed somewhat silly to Brian, especially considering she was only next door. "Maybe I'll just go on over."

"No. Don't do that. She told you to call, right?"

"Yes."

"Then that's what she wants you to do. Let her set the parameters. She wants to feel comfortable with you, so give her every reason to."

Brian nodded.

Helen ended the call soon after. Brian wondered if he should have even told her about the date. Here he was, a grown man, telling his sister about his romantic conquests.

Telling his sister about *Her*.

At least he wouldn't tell her about the man throwing stones at the window the other night or the note through the door. Last thing Helen needed was another reason to worry about him.

That note . . .

That man . . .

Were they connected somehow? And what did 'get out' even mean? A threat or a well-intentioned warning? Either way, Brian didn't appreciate it. Much as he hadn't appreciated vinyl trousers shooting him those dagger eyes. Lexie had assured Brian this was a good town, full of good people, but Brian wasn't so sure about either.

━ク│ヽ━

Brian cursed the silent living room when the realisation hit—he still hadn't picked up coffee and eggs. He'd headed all the way into town only to wind up talking to Lexie and forget about the original point of the trip. Brian knew he wasn't exactly in his prime, but surely he shouldn't be suffering from amnesia. He wasn't *that* old. He grabbed his jacket and slipped on a pair of trainers, leaving the apartment as quickly as possible, lest he forget again.

Outside there was an orange glow to the dusking sky and the evening air smelt crisp. Brian took a deep breath, filling up his lungs, and savouring the moment. Perhaps there really was something to the whole 'sea air is good for you' claim. He proceeded out of the residents' car park, turning left and down the road towards the corner shop he'd visited earlier that week. He expected he'd wind up spending more money on lower quality products, but that was the literal and metaphorical price to pay for his shitty memory.

About halfway to the shop, Brian heard fast footsteps and light panting behind him. He moved to the right side of the pavement and slowed his pace to allow whoever was in such a hurry to overtake, but

64

when thirty seconds elapsed and no one had passed, he glanced around. There was nobody about. Just a thick stretch of road and the progressively darkening sky. He shook his head and zipped up his jacket, the temperature plummeting—a chill pinched his neck.

A bell chimed to signal Brian's arrival as he entered the corner shop. It was cramped inside—aisles barely wide enough for a single person—and the place stank of McDonald's, which seemed strange until Brian noticed the carton of fries and burger on the countertop. A broadsheet newspaper mostly obscured the cashier's face. Though Brian couldn't see much, he knew the cashier was different from the first time he'd visited. For one, he could make out a charcoal black beard which he was fairly sure the young blonde woman was incapable of growing at all, let alone in around a week, and for another, the guy was at least twice the size of her and double her age. The cashier rested his legs on the countertop, heavy work boots next to the fast food.

"Evening," Brian said, his voice an octave lower than usual, trying to sound friendly and masculine, neither of which came naturally.

The cashier, who he figured was likely the owner due to his age, didn't even grunt. Well, whatever, Brian soon located the eggs. Some brand he'd never heard of before, housed in a blue cardboard box—a smiling anthropomorphised egg stood on the front, flexing its hulking bicep.

He held the egg carton up in the air and looked over at the shop owner. "It's good that is—eat your eggs and you, too, will have egg-cellent physique." The owner didn't react. "*Egg*-cellent because . . ."

Brian moved onto the coffee, the choices of which ranged from bad to worse. Brian sure as hell wasn't buying the freeze-dried instant crap which, personally, he thought had no business being called coffee in the first place, but the one packet of ground coffee they did have looked like a Starbucks rip-off and he figured it would play havoc with his stomach.

"You got anything single-origin or Fairtrade?" Brian called over to the owner.

This time the owner put his newspaper down and huffed out air. He ran a hand through his greased back ponytailed hair.

The two locked eyes.

"The coffee," Brian said. "I don't suppose you have anything that's Fairtrade?"

"Fair fucking what?" The man sounded as friendly as he looked.

Brian lowered his head. "It's just, it can be difficult choosing the right coffee, know what I mean?"

"No. I don't."

Brian picked up the Starbucks rip-off, shook it, as if in doing so he might unearth some secret.

"What you see is what you get," the owner said.

Brian placed the eggs and coffee on the counter. He looked up at the security camera in the upper righthand corner. Fish motifs, not too dissimilar from the ones around his apartment building, were emblazoned on the camera's exterior. The owner caught Brian looking.

"Looks familiar," Brian said.

"So?"

Brian hadn't expected that response. He changed tack. "On my way here, I could have sworn someone was behind me, but when I turned around there was nobody there. Weird, huh?"

The owner scanned the goods, bagged them up, and motioned to the electronic display indicating the grand total. Brian handed him a tenner and the owner returned some change. Brian wondered if the owner could be the same man who'd loitered outside Yuki's apartment. They both had a beard and long hair, so it was possible, but he wasn't so sure about the build. Brian looked away—he'd been staring.

The owner cleared his throat. "Yes? Can I help you with anything else?"

Brian wasn't sure. He glanced at the security camera—the fish were freaking him out.

"Fuck me, are you really not gonna leave until I answer your stupid question?" the owner said. "All right, fine. No, it isn't weird you heard someone behind you one minute and they weren't there the next. There are many streets, many houses, too. Whoever you heard, they turned off, they went down some other road or whatever. Fuck me, son, are you *that* dense?"

Despite the owner's tone, Brian was relieved. It made sense.

"Do me a favour, yeah?" the owner said, and Brian went to answer but the owner got there first. "Fuck off."

As Brian left the shop, he noticed all the other cameras—each covered in fish motifs, each pointed towards him, each watching him.

><

Back home, Brian warmed a can of soup on the stove. He wasn't hungry but had to eat something. He was too wound up and jittery. About Yuki, about the man in the shop, about the roaming fish eyes, about the footsteps he could have sworn he'd heard behind him. He was losing it. He'd heard the old cliché about love doing funny things to people, but he wasn't so sure this was the kind of *funny* it meant. *Love* . . . holy shit, where was his head at? They'd shared coffee and a kiss on the cheek. It barely constituted a date, let alone love. Brian needed to calm down before calling Yuki later. He poured himself a large measure of whiskey and sat on the sofa, playing with his phone. Yuki's number was in his contacts, he just needed to press 'call'. His finger hovered over his phone whilst he considered what to say. Why did it matter? As usual, he was overthinking things. He put down the phone and walked over to the bedroom window to check her car was parked outside. For some reason, he felt like he needed her to be home to talk. If she was out, then he probably wouldn't have her undivided attention.

Blue light flickered from beyond the curtains. Was there an ambulance at the apartment? Brian parted the curtains just enough to look outside and immediately saw the light's source.

All the fish statues around the car park were lit— blue flames wavering in the breeze. Funny, Brian hadn't seen any vans or workers around. Perhaps someone had done the work whilst he was in town. Regardless, it added an air of sophistication, classing up the entire complex.

THEY'RE WATCHING

Brian looked to Yuki's parking space, saw her car and the man standing next to it, staring up at her apartment.

He backed away from the window.

It was him. The bloke from the other night. Brian was sure of it.

Crouching down, Brian peeked through the blinds again. The man wore dark clothes just as before. Standing motionless, staring straight ahead.

Who was this man?

Brian stayed low and crab-walked over to his front door, sliding the deadlock across slowly. With the door locked, he didn't feel any more secure.

He needed to call Yuki.

He stared at his phone on the sofa.

What if the man was one of her ex-boyfriends? What if she knew he was watching her, but her plan was to ignore him until he went away? That didn't seem likely. But it was possible. They hadn't spoken about past relationships and it was hardly the kind of thing she'd bring up on a first date. There was so much about *Her* he didn't know.

Brian clenched his fists. This man was disrupting everything. Brian stood up. Was there anything in the apartment he could use as a weapon? Not to hurt the man, just to scare him off for good. A thousand scenarios played through Brian's mind. He risked a peek through the blinds again and found the man pacing behind Yuki's car.

Brian kept a large chef's knife in his cutlery drawer, but it was too obvious. He wanted to surprise the man, and that meant going outside. But not through the main entrance. He could leave through the fire exit at the back, walk around the side of the building, and approach the man that way.

He put down the chef's knife and picked up a paring knife. Though the blade was only four inches long, it could do quite a bit of damage, just in case he needed it for self-defence.

As Brian was preparing to leave, he heard a hiss from behind. He shot round, knife ready, fearing the worst. He relaxed when he saw it was just the soup bubbling over and spilling onto the stove. He placed the pan on the kitchen countertop. No time to eat now.

Grabbing his phone from the sofa, then the keys from the counter, Brian left his apartment and headed outside.

ELEVEN

AS BRIAN APPROACHED the front of the building, he could hear the man pacing the car park. His shoes were loud, clicking on the pavement. Brian watched, waiting for the right moment to sneak out and get behind his own car.

The man stopped pacing. He looked back over at Yuki's apartment, then turned and started walking away. Brian crouched low and slid behind his car. He looked through the passenger wing mirror as the man exited the car park. He ambled away, as though he had no particular place to go.

Does he know I saw him?

The man didn't turn around. Brian stood, then followed. He kept his eyes on the man, walking at a relaxed and measured pace. The knife lay in Brian's back trouser pocket, blade up, so he'd have to be careful if he needed to grab it. When he made it halfway across the car park, the overhead lights went out. All at once.

Only the light from the fish statues and the pale moon remained.

Unusually pale. Sickly pale.

The sky was clear, no clouds obscuring his view, and yet the moon looked like a faded photo of itself.

It was large and glowing and appeared unrealistic. Hyperrealistic even. There wasn't much moonlight, and the man was barely visible as he reached the tall grass beyond the car park. As far as Brian knew there was nothing but fields for miles, if he wanted to get anywhere he should have stuck to the pavement, at least that way he'd make it to town if he walked long enough.

Brian followed, his eyes never straying from the man. When Brian walked onto the grass, he chanced a look back at Pelagic Court. The fish torches illuminated the front of the buildings, casting grim shadows that ebbed and flowed around the light. He looked away and back to the man. He could still see him walking through the field. Squinting, Brian noticed what appeared to be a small subdivision past the field, a residential tract that reminded Brian of photos he'd seen of American suburbanite dwellings.

Brian pressed on after the man.

Cautious.

Patient.

The ground was dry, but Brian's shoes still found all the spots damp with dew. If they were more inland, the field would have been covered with fog.

Stay off the moors.

Yes, he did feel a little like an American out of place, but nowhere near London, and definitely not a werewolf. His mind kept telling him he needed to turn back, to go right up to Yuki's door and pound on it until she opened up. But then, the man would come back, wouldn't he?

No, he needed to end this.

Tonight.

THEY'RE WATCHING

As he drew nearer, Brian confirmed that there was indeed a concrete subdivision—a residential estate that separated one field from another. Standing at the edge of the tall grass, Brian stopped to watch the man's next move. He walked down the main road, which ended in a cul-de-sac, with three streets branching off of it. The streetlights were bright, too bright for him to follow any closer. Brian stepped onto the street. He felt vulnerable. *Exposed.* Completely out in the open under the streetlight. He dashed into the shadows and continued to follow the man.

The man skipped the first street but turned down the second. Cautious of triggering security light sensors, Brian remained as far from driveways as possible. The wind had picked up, and as he crept closer to the man, things in the air stung his eyes.

The sub-division was still under construction, with most of the homes on the second street incomplete. Giant mounds of dirt and sand filled a few of the gardens and driveways, the strong wind kicking up grit. The man continued to walk at an even pace and eventually turned up the driveway to the last house on the left.

For the shortest of moments, Brian chuckled to himself. This was no time to be thinking about old Wes Craven films.

TWELVE

WHILST MANY OF the houses were new builds under construction, this one had seen better days. Not exactly dilapidated, but it appeared abandoned—like some of the places Brian had seen overtaken by squatters in inner cities, the type of places you didn't visit during the day, let alone at night. Luckily this wasn't the city, there was no one about to give him trouble, and yet every fibre in Brian's body told him to get the hell out of there, *now.*

Brian stayed put. He'd trudged this far, might as well stick around a little longer.

For what, you idiot? You know where he lives. Time to get moving!

But Brian doubted the man lived there—it didn't look inhabitable. And yet upon arriving the man had taken a key from his pocket, unlocked the door, and headed inside. Seconds later lights had illuminated the downstairs window—at least there was electricity.

Brian watched from behind the van on the driveway opposite. Luckily the last house on the right was still under construction, so no one would open the front door and interrogate him, demanding he get the hell off their property, or worse. And if someone did come along, well, Brian would deal with that when it happened.

Five minutes passed and Brian swore he heard someone breathing. He shot around, but all he saw was a half-built house. He surveyed the area, as best he could—given the whole 'hiding behind a van' predicament—but came up empty. There was no one else about. And besides, even if there was, they'd have to be crouching right next to him for Brian to hear their breathing. The thought did little to calm Brian's nerves. The wind howled into the night as if providing an answer. He'd heard nothing but the wind's song, his mind painting make-belief spaces with imaginary colour.

Ten minutes passed. The man remained inside. Perhaps the man *did* live there. Sure, the place looked ready for demolition and sharply contrasted with the rest of the buildings in the area, but there could be a perfectly decent reason for that. Perhaps the property had sentimental value, had belonged to a now deceased grand-relative and nobody in the man's family had the heart to sell it.

Brian stared at the building, the more he drank in, the more it frightened him, as if the bricks themselves were staring back. Challenging him to make a move. Fucking daring him.

It was possible the man had turned in for the night. Was Brian really going to camp out and wait? To what cnd? To confront the man? To make his way inside the house? To track the man until he understood why he'd been following Yuki, what relationship he had to her, whether he posed a threat? The more Brian considered his options, the more ridiculous he realised

75

his behaviour. He'd followed the man on a whim, but there'd been no strategy, no next step. He was making it up as he went along. Thing was, the entire area was so isolated, Brian felt that if he backtracked, he'd make a noise and then the man would look out of the window and see him and . . .

And then what, dumbass? And then he's going to come after you and kill you? This isn't actually *a Wes Craven film, this is some creepy man who throws stones at windows, he has his peculiarities and probably has his reasons, too . . . You know, like you—a creepy man who peeps through holes in the wall.*

The building was glaring at him now. Its scars and wounds winking at Brian. Taunting him. He wouldn't give in. Wouldn't make a stupid decision because the building wanted him to. Brian was a lot of things but impatient was not one of them. He made his decision, he'd wait until the man made a move even if he had to stay out there all night.

➤⟍╎⟋➤

Luckily for Brian, he didn't have to stay out there all night. Fifteen minutes later and the man was out of the house, carrying a small cardboard box. The man walked away from the house and down the street a few hundred metres until he came to a badly parked car, one wheel on the kerb. It was the definition of an old banger, 1980s build with a smattering of rust evenly distributed. The man rested the package on the bonnet as he unlocked the car, before throwing the box on the backseat, and getting into the car. It took a few turns of the ignition key for the car to start, but once it did the engine roared to life and exhaust fumes filled the air. After which, it was foot to the floor, and the man sped off. Wherever he was going he wasn't being subtle about it in a noisy piece-of-shit car like that.

What if he'd led me here as a distraction? To get me away from the apartment so he could have Yuki to himself? But that made little sense, had no logic to it. The man looked like he could handle himself and wouldn't shy away from confrontation. If he'd genuinely seen Brian, he'd have likely approached. *"The fuck you following me for?"* Brian was glad it hadn't come to that because he'd have given him a piece of his mind, too, and asked him what the bloody hell he was playing at snooping around the apartments.

Brian waited a few minutes, then edged out from behind the van and made his way towards the last house on the left. He hadn't seen the man lock-up—might as well head inside and see what's what, see if there were any clues as to who the man was and what he was doing. It didn't quite align with Brian's own perception of himself, the whole trespassing on other people's property, but neither did stalking strange men, or spying on beautiful women.

He tried the door.

No such luck.

Brian made his way around the back of the house which was easy enough. There was no fence or gate or indeed anything to separate front from back.

Was this too easy? Was the house or the man or some amalgam of the two tricking Brian? He shook his head. He couldn't think like that. His job was to get inside and investigate, not to waste time worrying about the absurd.

The back garden comprised of overgrown grass, weeds, and litter. Discarded beer cans, broken glass, a couple of orange and white traffic cones, and even a supermarket trolley—minor traps and obstacles for Brian to navigate around. At the furthest end of the garden, away from everything else, stood a child's swing—rusted metal and old wood, rocking backwards-and-forwards, screeching in the wind. *Ugh!* Brian wanted no part of that. He didn't scare easily but there was something about neglected children's toys that creeped him out.

It looked like someone else had got curious about the house—cobwebs glossed the door's perimeter, but the pane gazing into the kitchen had been shattered. Brian checked the door wasn't already unlocked, then reached his arm through the pane, careful to avoid jagged glass, and felt for a lock. Eventually he found a simple latch and slid it back.

"I wouldn't, if I were you," a deep voice said from behind.

Brian removed his shaking arm from the windowpane, almost scraping himself along the broken edges.

"Stay put," the voice said.

Brian figured it had to be the man. Perhaps he'd caught onto Brian following him—speeding off had been a ruse to see what Brian would do next, but really, he'd parked his banged-up motor around the corner and returned to the house. He knew this shit was too good to be true. The watcher becoming the watched.

THEY'RE WATCHING

Footsteps trudged towards Brian.

What the hell would the man do when he caught up with Brian? If he called the police that would likely be the end of Brian's new job—fired before he'd even begun. Though given the man's previous behaviour—throwing stones up at the window, loitering around the apartment complex, perhaps even pushing that threatening note through Brian's door—he didn't reckon he was the type to go the legal route.

Brian had to act and fast, before the man did.

"Easy now, son," the man said, grabbing Brian from behind. "Don't move."

But Brian did move, mustering up all his strength he broke free. He fumbled for the paring knife in his back pocket but couldn't quite grasp it. He swivelled to meet the man.

The only thing Brian met with was a headbutt rocking him to the floor.

Pain squawked throughout his skull and specks of light danced across his vision. Brian retched, his throat stinging. The man grabbed Brian by the scruff of his neck and half-led, half-dragged Brian away from the house. Brian tried swinging a leg towards the man but wobbled—the only damage delivered was scuffed footwear courtesy of the concrete. The more Brian struggled, the more the man's grip on him tightened, so he let himself fall limp, relenting to the man, as he blindly followed, the world in front of him foggy and discombobulated.

An electronic bleep snapped Brian to attention.

Fresh panic flooded his body as he registered what was happening, but before his body had time to react he was heaved up and dumped into the boot of the car.

THIRTEEN

DARKNESS ENGULFED BRIAN and his body ached in places he hadn't known existed. Head throbbing, thoughts spinning, as he swerved from side-to-side—vibrations jarring his already fragile frame. His perception and reality twisted and for a moment he thought he'd died and gone to hell. A bit harsh, all considered. He'd not been a model citizen—peeping on women, getting close to Lexie when he already had something going with *Her*, then the whole—

Oh, Christ. *Her*! Was she okay?

Thoughts of Yuki jolted Brian back to reality, the sound of AC/DC's 'Back in Black' booming over the roar of the car engine confirmed his suspicions. He was not in hell, but in the boot of some car. He hadn't really seen the vehicle, the evening's darkness and scattered stars scrambling his eyesight, but most likely it was that piece-of-shit banger the man had been driving before he'd nutted him. What else was he capable of? It was better for Brian to strike first, an anticipatory shot. He reached for the paring knife which, despite the kerfuffle, was still tucked in his back pocket. His luck ended there, every time he got close, the car turned hard. The guy was probably driving along backroads, zigzagging to some place out in the sticks. Did he plan on killing Brian? Panicked and flooded with adrenaline, Brian stretched for the knife once more but wound up bending his index finger backwards, inflicting further pain. He took a deep breath, inhaling unwashed gym clothes and stale cigarettes—between that and the movement, Brian was in danger of hurling. He swallowed, concentrating on his breath, slow and shallow, counting to twenty.

Soon Brian felt less nauseous, willing himself to think logically. The man wasn't gonna kill him—if that was the case, he'd already be dead. Besides, Brian hadn't done anything *that* wrong. Sure, he shouldn't have followed the man and he definitely shouldn't have gone snooping around the back of his house, but he hadn't entered the house and hadn't stolen anything either. His biggest mistake had been reaching for the knife—thank lord he hadn't got that far, whatever the outcome, he'd have been in a much worse predicament. As far as Brian gathered, the man didn't even know about the knife, he'd just intercepted a trespasser—some would-be burglar who'd refused to cooperate—which was why the man had been physical. As soon as the two got to talking they'd straighten things out, perhaps in years to come they could even laugh about it.

Brian almost found comfort in his bullshit narrative. Then he snapped back to reality.

If the guy was so harmless, why had he lamped Brian in the head and locked him in the boot of his car?

Trickier to explain, but not impossible. This was just a citizen's arrest, the man was taking him to the nearest police station and—well, shit, if that was his plan there went Brian's job, his future, his chance with *Her*.

Brian had to stop him at all costs. To retrieve the knife. To do what needed to be done.

◄╱▮╲►

By the time the engine stopped, Brian was psyched up and ready to go. With the car now still, Brian scrambled to the knife. He held it close to his chest, readying himself for the big moment. As soon as the guy opened the boot Brian would pounce. He'd never stabbed anyone before, had barely even punched someone, unless you included playground fights where he'd got his arse kicked, which Brian didn't, but how hard could it be? Brian had watched *The Warriors* several times and completed both *Streets of Rage* and *Golden Axe* on the Sega MegaDrive—he reckoned he could handle himself in a life or death situation.

The boot opened and streetlight stung Brian's eyes. He started squinting, which hadn't been part of the plan, but still managed to lift himself up, his joints cracking in the process.

"What in the—" the man started, but Brian didn't let him finish, waving the knife towards him.

The man caught it, blade first, cutting his palm. "You, motherfucker!" With the knife still gripped in his bloodied right hand, the man threw a left elbow into Brian's nose, then shoved a knee into his doughy stomach. Brian folded to the floor, wailing hard as if still being beaten. Brian kicked and punched invisible enemies, sprawled out on the concrete.

"Are you quite done?"

82

THEY'RE WATCHING

Brian stared up at the man, went to talk, but instead of words his screaming resumed. The man bent down, putting his left hand over Brian's mouth, forcing him to splutter as if suffocating.

"Get a hold of yourself, son. I'm not here to hurt you. I just want to talk."

The man removed his hand from Brian's mouth.

"Talk? Then why the fuck did you attack me?"

"I told you not to move."

"You *headbutted* me."

"And you just busted my hand, you fucking idiot." The man raised his hand, still holding the knife. "There's blood everywhere. What's wrong with you?"

"I thought you were gonna kill me."

"Based on what?"

Brian got up. Standing this close to the man, with the streetlight illuminating his face, Brian could tell this wasn't the same bloke who'd thrown stones at the window. This was *not* the man he'd followed to that rundown house. Though he had a similar beard—thick and dense with hardly any patches—this guy had much shorter hair, clean and slick. He wore a leather jacket that looked almost new and tailored black trousers—a far cry from what the other man had sported. Brian glanced back at the car—a black BMW, a few decades newer than the old banger. It was parked outside an old manor house—though, unlike the house he'd seen earlier, this was in good nick. The type of house Brian imagined Fitzgerald's Gatsby or some millionaire artist owning. There were no other houses or people in sight.

The guy tucked the knife in his pocket, then clasped his fist tightly shut.

"Can I—" Brian began.

"You want me to give you your knife back?"

Brian nodded.

"How stupid do you think I am, kid?"

"I—"

"Don't answer that." The man reached into his inner jacket pocket, Brian flinched, looking visibly relieved when the man merely proffered a packet of cigarettes. "You want one or not?"

"I th-thought it was a gun."

The man arched an eyebrow. "You're a strange one, son. And fine, suit yourself." The man put a cigarette in his mouth, returning the packet to his pocket, before sparking up.

Brian caught a whiff of the man's cologne—overpowering and masculine, probably with a name like Brute or Savage or perhaps even Bastard.

Brian watched the man closely, there was something familiar about him that Brian couldn't quite place. The man noticed Brian staring—he didn't say anything but appeared unsettled. Brian straightened up, scratching the back of his neck.

"Wait a minute," Brian said. "I've seen you before."

The man shrugged. "And?"

"In the supermarket . . . we bumped into each other."

The man narrowed his eyes. "Are you the prick that wasn't watching where he was going? You should be more careful."

That wasn't the way Brian remembered it, more like the other way around, though he didn't correct him.

"Is that what this is about?" Brian asked.

"You think I started following you because you're incapable of walking like a normal human being?" The man cleared his throat. "I'm a PI."

"A PI . . . Like a private investigator?"

"What other type of PI do you know?"

"There's the number but . . . Wait a minute, what kind of private investigator goes around headbutting people?" Brian stuffed his hands deep into his pockets. "Can I see some ID?"

"No, you cannot."

"Then how am I supposed to—"

"Because I told you, already."

"So, I'm just meant to believe you?"

"I don't see that you have any other choice."

Brian looked at the PI's hand. He was still bleeding. Brian went to say something but didn't want to draw attention to the damage he'd inflicted.

"What's your name?" Brian asked.

"Ted."

"Ted what?"

"Just Ted. That's all you need to know. Truth be told, you don't need to know that, but I'm feeling courteous. Now, please, let's step inside. I have some questions." He gestured to the manor house.

"What if I want to stay out here?" Brian shivered, the evening's chill setting in, his actions betraying his words.

"Oh sure, you look *very* comfortable. And besides, the subject matter's a little sensitive, I think we'd be better off inside."

As if I'm gonna trust some guy who forced me into a car and drove me all the way out here . . .

Ted beckoned Brian closer. "Now, come on. It's freezing out here and there's whiskey inside, but hey, if you'd rather we do it out here, that's not a problem. Believe me, I've had far worse working conditions. Things you couldn't begin to imagine." Ted stepped closer. "Still, it's a *very* nice bottle of whiskey. Woodford Reserve Double Oaked Kentucky straight bourbon."

"Wait, it's a bourbon?"

Ted grinned. "Oh, so now I've got your attention, huh?"

"I suppose it is a *little* cold."

"It's funny, seems whenever I mention the whiskey it gets so bitterly cold around here." Ted turned towards the house. "Come on, follow me."

He led Brian through the hallway and to a sitting room adorned with avant-garde artwork. It wasn't quite what Brian had expected but he sure appreciated the open fire.

"Now, if you'll excuse me for a moment, I've got to take care of my damn hand."

Ted soon returned, right hand bandaged up, a smile on his face, and a spring in his step. He didn't look like the type of person who was gonna go around hurting people.

Yeah but neither did Bundy . . .

"Please, take a seat."

Brian sat on a dark brown leather chair whilst Ted fixed the drinks. He handed Brian a generously sized glass of whiskey, planting the bottle on the table between them before settling down with his own glass.

Brian drank. "Jesus, that's smooth!"

THEY'RE WATCHING

"You can really taste the cherries, huh? And the vanilla and caramel are just . . . " Ted kissed the air. "But, look, we're not here to review whiskey, let's get down to business. There's a person of interest, some nasty piece of work I've been keeping tabs on for the last couple of weeks. The guy's volatile and believed to be highly dangerous." Ted poured more whiskey, first for Brian, then for himself. "So, my question to you is this, what business do you have with him?"

Brian frowned. "I'm sorry but I—"

"You followed him all the way from your apartment to his house. As far as I could tell he was unaware. Then you hid, waiting for him to leave, before you made your move. What do you know?"

Brian swigged the whiskey, hoping it would help, but even the sweet liquor offered no comfort. "I followed him because he—"

"You weren't planning on carrying out some vigilante justice, were you?"

"Me? Of course not. Why would you—"

Ted's eyes narrowed. "Come on, son, you were armed. I should know." He held up his bandaged hand.

"It was for protection, in case things got out of hand."

"So, you often go around stabbing people if they step out of line?"

"What? No! I just—"

"I'll ask you again, what do you know about him?"

"Nothing. I know nothing. That's the point."

"I don't buy it. You don't stalk someone you know nothing about."

MICHAEL DAVID WILSON & BOB PASTORELLA

Brian grimaced. *Stalk* wasn't right. That made him sound predatory. He thought of *Her* and began to doubt himself. Was he the bad guy after all? He'd been doing this for him and *Her*. But mostly *Her*.

"Time for you to talk," Ted said.

"I'm no stalker," Brian said, lowering his head.

"Then help me understand what you are. What's your relationship to him?"

Brian breathed deeply. "We have no relationship, not really. He keeps turning up at the apartment complex."

"Why?"

"That's what I was trying to figure out."

"By stalking him."

Brian's lips twisted in revulsion. "Not the smartest move, I know, but I had to do something. He just kept staring up at *Her* window."

"Whose window?"

Fuck. He hadn't mentioned her by name, but perhaps in saying as much as he had, he'd betrayed *Her*. What if there was some secret between her and the man? Something innocent that explained everything. Or what if he was blackmailing her? If the very things Brian was saying were putting her life in danger.

"Someone else lives at the complex," Ted said.

Not sure if it was a question or statement, Brian concentrated on keeping his lips tightly shut.

"A woman, right?" Ted folded his arms. "Athletic, long hair—"

"She's got nothing to do with this!"

Ted sat forward. "So, you *do* know something."

"No, it's just she would ne-never do anything like that."

"Like *what*?"

Sweat dripped down Brian's forehead.

"Never do anything like *what*?"

Brian shrugged. "I'm just saying, she's a good person, that's all."

"Hmm . . . See, as far as I understand it, you're new to the area. So, that being the case, how do you know so much about her?"

Brian kept quiet.

"Did you know her *before* moving?"

Brian scratched his wrist. "I didn't but sometimes you just get a sense about someone, don't you? You just know."

"Not in my line of work you don't. D.T.A. Don't trust anyone." Ted sipped his whiskey. "Now, just so I'm clear on your involvement or lack thereof, what you're telling me is you noticed this guy snooping around the apartments and then tonight you had enough and decided to follow him back to his, that about the size of it?"

"He'd been throwing stones at the windows," Brian said, unsure if that made him sound more justified or crazier.

"You really don't know anything about this guy, do you?"

Brian shook his head.

"Best you keep it that way," Ted said. "Hold up a minute, the moment I saw you, were you really about to break into his house?"

"The windowpane was already shattered when I got there."

"Right, so I didn't catch you about to unlock the door?"

Brian blushed. "None of this makes much sense. I'm just an honest guy and I want to help but you have to tell me what's going on here."

"An honest guy, huh?"

"That's right."

"Uh-huh." Ted crossed his arms. "I'm not sure I believe you, like I said, *don't trust anyone*, but I can't say you're much of a threat either. So, here's the deal, there's been a number of missing people over the past few years, mostly out-of-towners, loners, that kind of thing, and I'm investigating."

Ted refilled Brian's whiskey glass without breaking eye contact. Brian picked up the glass to drink but put it back down when he realised Ted was waiting for him to speak. Was this a technique Ted used to coerce confessions out of people?

"Like you said, I just moved to the area. I doubt I would know anything about missing people."

Ted scratched his chin. "Do you?"

"I mean, no, at least I don't think I do . . . "

"Seems you're not so sure."

"Well . . . "

"Let me lay things out for you, really simple, so you understand. I've only recently been brought in, though I've been aware of this for some time now, everyone around here has, not that people will tell you that, everyone wants to pretend this town is safe, like if they keep quiet and ignore it, the problem will just go away. But it won't."

"This town isn't safe?"

Ted reclined back in his chair. "Show me a town that truly is."

"When I was living in Warwick—"

THEY'RE WATCHING

"Stop. The hell's wrong with you? Always answering non-questions."

"I just—"

"Point is, no town is safe. No place is safe. It's just some disguise it better than others. They create an illusion of safety, but mark my words, son, it *is* an illusion."

"This isn't exactly making me feel comfortable."

"Oh, really? Maybe you should put your feet up on the table here. Or perhaps you can drink the whiskey from the bottle if you'll feel more at home." Ted slammed a fist down on the table. "Don't you dare. This isn't a fucking holiday camp or some cosy sleepover between friends. And it sure as shit isn't my job to make you feel comfortable. This is serious, you understand?"

Brian clasped his hands together.

"The sister of one of the missing people brought me in," Ted said. "She didn't think the police were doing a good enough job in finding her brother— either because they weren't taking things seriously enough or . . . well, she reckons there might be something more sinister at play."

"Like an inside job?"

Ted lit another cigarette. He didn't offer Brian one this time, but he pushed the open packet and lighter to the centre of the table should Brian want one later.

"Perhaps," Ted said. "At this stage, I'm investigating all possibilities."

"What's your take on the police around here? You don't think they're good enough either?"

"I didn't say that. But what I will say is the missing bloke's been gone almost a year now. I'll leave you to draw your own conclusions," Ted said. "Now this sister, she has a lot of money and she's persistent, too—wants to see results and fast. Older sisters can be very protective. Believe me, I know."

Brian swallowed. "I wonder why it took her a year to seek you out. I mean, if she's that protective, why—"

"I'm not exactly cheap, son. Besides, put yourself in her situation. Imagine someone you care about goes missing—you gonna go to the police or a PI first?"

"I guess the police but—"

"Exactly. They only come to me when they get desperate, which in recent years has been a lot more often than I'm used to."

"Good for business."

"Bad for all concerned." Ted smirked. "Anyway, I think I've heard all I need to hear from you, it's pretty clear you know nothing about this man, and if you're smart, you'll keep it that way." Ted massaged his jawline. "As far as that neighbour of yours goes, maybe she's involved, maybe she isn't."

"She isn't."

"Well, that's for me to decide. I need to keep a close eye on the both of them."

"You're gonna spy on her?"

"I'm a private *investigator*, son. Aren't you following along? You suffering from amnesia or something?"

"I just don't think it's right that you spy on her, is all."

"Okay, well, frankly I couldn't give a shit what you do or don't think about me and my job. I'm not interested in your approval. I'm interested in the truth."

"*Her* is truth."

"What's that?"

"*Her* would never do anything wrong."

"The fuck are you talking about?" Ted gritted his teeth so hard, he was in danger of scraping off the enamel.

"*Her*."

"Yuki?"

Brian felt sick. "How do you know her name?"

"Same way I know yours, Brian. This is my job." Ted reached into his trouser pocket and pulled out a card which he passed to Brian. "I believe our business is done here. If you think of anything else that might be of interest or if you see anything, get in touch *immediately*."

Brian eyed up the Woodford Reserve.

"Don't push your luck," Ted said, rising.

Brian stood and the two shook hands.

"I'll call you a taxi," Ted said. "And don't worry about the cost, it's on me."

"Right. Well, thanks, I guess, and, um, sorry about your hand."

"Just a flesh wound." Ted stepped so close Brian could smell the whiskey on him. "Now, one more thing about the woman, Yuki, I wondered if you could keep an eye on her, just in case."

"You want me to peep?"

Ted squinted. "That's a weird way of putting it."

"I could never do that," Brian said. "I'm not a peeper."

"Sure— I never said you were, but if you wouldn't mind, you know . . . "

Brian surely did know, and he wanted no part of it.

"Well, then, I'll call that taxi unless—"

"There was a note," Brian said. "Someone pushed it through my letterbox the first day I arrived. It said, 'Get Out'."

"Not the friendliest of neighbours then," Ted said so nonchalantly, Brian thought he might be suppressing a laugh.

"You're not concerned?"

"It's nothing to worry about."

"Well, it did worry me. To be honest, the fact you don't seem worried is worrying me, too."

"I get that. You seem like a worrier," Ted said.

"What would you do if you were me?"

"I wouldn't do anything."

"Because?"

"Listen, son, it's just a note. It could be one of several things, nothing to concern yourself with."

"Such as?"

"Honestly, my best guess is it's either an angry local or the sister who put me onto this case in the first place. Like I told you, she's persistent and she's been trying to warn people about 'the dangers of this town', her words not mine. What can I say? Her methods are unconventional."

"You think it was her?"

"Maybe, maybe not. Wouldn't be the first time she's pulled something like that. But, as I said, an angry local is just as likely."

"They hate outsiders?"

"Not exactly. That apartment block you're living in used to be council houses. Some rich developer came in and the whole lot got knocked down, a lot of people lost their houses, and now they're just swanky apartments for rich folk."

"Is that even legal?"

"It's what happened. Anyway, don't take the note personally, there's just a lot of people rubbed up the wrong way—you're lucky it was a note and not a brick. I don't suppose you still have the note, do you?"

Brian had it somewhere, but he didn't want to give it to some PI. "I'm not sure I do."

A car pulled up outside the manor house.

"Looks like your taxi's here," Ted said, which Brian thought strange, he could have sworn Ted hadn't called one yet. "You take care of yourself, son." Ted opened the front door. "And stay safe."

FOURTEEN

WHEN **BRIAN RETURNED** home, he rushed towards the peephole to check on Yuki. She did not dance that night, but she slept. And Brian watched.

FIFTEEN

UPON **WAKING**, Brian found himself slumped on the floor inside the open wardrobe, a stack of towels served as a makeshift pillow. Mud and grass flecked up his trousers, burrs clung to his shirt, and his scalp itched from god knows what.

After a thorough shower and quick breakfast, Brian left the apartment, headed for town. He wanted to grab a proper cup of coffee and tell Lexie about what had gone down the previous night. Brian wasn't sure he understood everything that had happened but seeing as Lexie had been the first to mention an unsolved case, he figured if anyone could help make sense of things it was her. Brian didn't know how much he'd end up telling Lexie but that wasn't important. His first concern was more coffee and shifting his alcohol-induced headache. Last night's bourbon might have been smooth, but Jesus Christ was he dealing with the aftermath.

In the car park, Brian lost his grip on his car keys a few steps from his Focus. They jangled on the concrete.

"You sure you should drive that?"

Brian looked up. Yuki was standing in front of her own car, an MX-5, gleaming red in the morning sunlight. He hadn't properly looked at her car before—even when they'd gone on their coffee date things had been a blur—but seeing their vehicles parked next to each other, Brian felt a wave of embarrassment. He forced a grin then retrieved his keys from the floor.

"Clumsy, huh?" It was the first time Brian had spoken that morning and it shot out like a choked bark.

"Whiskey will do that to you."

Bloody hell, did he still smell of it? Was he stumbling like a pisshead, too? He glanced at his hand to check his fingers weren't trembling.

"Or beer," Yuki said. "But you strike me as more of a whiskey man."

"That a good thing?"

Yuki winked. "What do you think?"

Brian hadn't a clue. He could barely string a sentence together before two strong cups of coffee, three on a hangover.

"So, I was thinking about our date the other day . . . " Yuki said.

Don't trust anyone. But he did trust Yuki, yet there was a part of him that questioned it. *Fuck.* Between talking to the PI and seeing Lexie, Brian was damn near cheating on *Her.*

"Hello? I said I was thinking about our date the other day." Yuki flipped her ponytail.

"Yeah, thanks for the coffee." The fuck was he going on about? Not only did that make no sense given he'd paid for it, but it sounded dismissive, as if he wanted to get away from *Her*, which maybe he did but he still . . . not *loved* her but something close.

THEY'RE WATCHING

"I mean, thanks for showing me the new coffee place." Brian adjusted his collar. "Not a new place but new to me."

"Why, of course. Maybe we could do it again sometime?"

She looked divine. Skin smooth, lips pouting, eyebrows freshly plucked. And she was initiating a second date. Yet Brian was glued to the spot, unable to react.

Keep an eye on her, just in case.

"Yuki, are you okay?" Brian's face deathly serious.

"The sun is out, yoga starts in half an hour, and the sea air is divine." She inhaled.

"Because if you weren't, if something or someone was bothering you, you could tell me."

"Sure." She flashed a smile, her teeth glimmering white. "And the same goes for you, mister Brian."

Electric excitement charged inside Brian. Even in his state of worry, she mesmerised him.

"When was the last time you *were* experiencing trouble?" Brian asked.

"Experiencing trouble." Yuki chewed over the words. "That's a funny way of putting it. But I like it. There's something a little magic realism. Maybe I should write a book about it."

"You write books?"

"Not yet, but one day. You might be my muse, Brian. I know you're my good luck charm. A few hours after our date I got a call from The Dolori Academy. I hadn't even applied, some talent scout tracked me down—he'd been keeping an eye on me."

"That a good thing?"

"Oh, it's no biggie, they're only the most prestigious dance academy in the universe. Just three locations. One in Italy, another in Germany, and the final one here in merry old England."

Brian looked to the floor. His boots muddied light brown from the previous night.

"So, when you say experiencing trouble . . . " Yuki beamed. "Damn, even saying it has that quality, you know?"

Brian didn't know. Hadn't a clue why his dumb phrasing had delighted her, but her positivity eased him. Maybe that was a bad thing, distracting him from the actual danger. Was there danger? Fuck, his head hurt. He trudged towards Yuki and colours rolled into a blur. He backtracked, putting his left hand out to steady himself against the car but missed. His legs skittered out of control and he fell forwards kissing the concrete.

❁

Lights and colours, sounds and smells, flickering back, painting reality. Yuki knelt next to Brian, holding his hand, telling him everything was okay.

"Yuki?"

"Shh. No need to talk, just concentrate on your breathing."

Brian's heart pounded. Breaths short and wheezy. He forced a long deep breath, exhaling slowly. His throat stung—sandpaper dry.

"Water?" Brian said.

Yuki squeezed his hand, then rushed over to her car. She returned with a bottle of Evian which Brian glugged in one. Yuki held his hand once more, her index finger stroking in soft circles, her gentle touch kissing and soothing. He concentrated on the sensation and Yuki's voice. Her accent healing.

100

"Should I call a doctor?"

Brian snapped to attention. "A doctor? What exactly—"

"Try not to speak unless you have to. One moment you were walking towards me, the next you were on the floor—you were out for a minute or so. When you came to you were having difficulty breathing. I think you may have had a panic attack."

"But I wasn't panicking . . . "

"A panic attack doesn't necessarily mean panicking. My mother used to have them when I was a kid, so I'm good at spotting the . . . Anyway, you don't need to worry yourself with any of that. How are you feeling?"

Brian's hands were twitching, matter of fact, so were his legs. "Better, I think, but strange. Like I'm shaking all over."

"Darling, you *are* shaking all over."

"I'll be fine." Brian made to stand.

Yuki helped him to his feet. "Slowly does it. Do you want to go inside for a bit? You can rest at mine, if you like?"

Brian couldn't impose himself. Not in *Her* sanctuary. "You've got your yoga class."

"You're more important than a stupid class. Now, about that doctor?"

"I'll be okay."

"You sure? I don't want you refusing because you're being all macho."

"I don't think I'm capable of being *all macho*. You really think I'm that type?"

Yuki laughed. "I dunno, Brian, you're full of surprises. A real man of mystery."

"Like Austin Powers?"

"*Way* better than Austin Powers."

"You don't like Austin Powers?"

Yuki took Brian's hand, even though he was steady and didn't need it. "I see you haven't lost your . . . " She paused for a moment, her hand not leaving his, her grip gentle, her skin soft and warm. "Well, you're still you."

"And that's a good thing?"

Yuki winked.

Their hands parted and Brian walked back to his car, taking the keys from his pocket. "I have to go."

"The only thing you have to do is look after yourself," Yuki said. "Though I'd like it if you told me what's bothering you."

Brian looked Yuki dead in the eye, went to tell her it was nothing, but was unable to do so. He could keep things from Yuki, could bend the truth, but a direct lie was not an option. That was worse than blasphemy.

"Come on, mister. I know there's *something* going on."

"Well, I did just have a *panic attack*," Brian mimed inverted commas as he said it.

"You did and it's serious. More serious than you're making out. But, look, I'm no idiot, I knew there was something up before that."

Brian wasn't sure if it was what Yuki had said or the aftermath of the attack, but his body felt hot all over. Last thing he wanted was for Yuki to think he was taking her for a fool. *Her* was divine knowledge and more, which meant . . . Which meant . . . Brian wobbled on the spot, but this time Yuki didn't react, so maybe it had been in his head, unless she was getting angry, her patience waning. Brian looked towards her. For guidance. For a sign. *Show me what to do.* For a split-second, Yuki seemed to react, and Brian wondered if he'd said it aloud, but her facial expression soon returned to cool-calm.

"I can't lie to you," Brian said.

"And you won't."

Did Yuki know of her own power? Not a request but a direct statement, an acknowledgement that to lie to *Her* would be an impossibility. Perhaps she already knew about the man with the stones and the PI but was just testing him. Waiting to see if he'd come clean.

What if she even knew about the peeping?

"So, I, erm . . . " Brian shuffled on the spot. How the fuck was he even gonna put it? "I care about you, Yuki. Like, *a lot.*"

Yuki nodded and Brian felt he could trust her. *Don't trust anyone*, was true enough. But Yuki wasn't anyone, she was *Her*. He'd tell her about the PI but would downplay it, omitting certain details.

"I ran into this geezer last night," Brian said. "Or maybe he ran into me. Either way, he was sniffing around the apartment complex, looking for clues and—"

"Clues?" Yuki raised an eyebrow.

"Right. Because he's investigating a guy—"

"What guy?"

"I dunno his name or anything, but—"

"What fucking guy?"

Brian had never seen her like this. Had he done something wrong?

MICHAEL DAVID WILSON & BOB PASTORELLA

"There's been a disappearance," Brian said.

"A kidnapping?"

"Nobody got kidnapped!" Now Brian was the one raising his voice.

Yuki took a step back.

"At least I don't think so. All I know is the guy's missing. Not the guy who was sniffing around or the guy he's investigating, but . . . but, there's a third guy. And that's the one who's missing."

"Wait, so how many people did you see last night?"

Fuck! If he said one it was a direct lie, but if he said two then shit got more complicated. Yuki filled the silence.

"When you say *investigating*, are we talking about a policeman or something else? Was this some sort of vigilante justice?"

Vigilante justice had been what the PI had said. Was that common in this town?

"He was a private investigator," Brian said.

Yuki recoiled, as if slugged in the face. Then she wiped sweat from her brow, threw her head back, and laughed. Brian figured she'd meant it to be cute, but the laugh went on too long—a mask to screen her discomfort.

"A private investigator isn't even a proper job. There are no licenses. Mostly it's just frustrated police officers or, worse still, people who couldn't hack police work to begin with." Yuki spoke with calm confidence. "What I don't get is why he was asking *you*. No offence, but you're not from around here, you've only just moved in."

"I guess it was a case of being in the right place at the right time . . . Or the wrong place. I didn't enjoy him grilling me."

104

"Was he aggressive? If he overstepped his boundaries, perhaps you should be the one going to the police about him."

"He was friendly enough . . . Concerned, even. He just wanted to know if I knew anything about this guy poking around the apartments."

"Someone's been—"

"It's nothing to worry about."

"Wait, so you've seen this guy the PI's investigating?"

"I don't know anything about the guy," Brian said, which was almost true.

"Should I be worried?"

Brian shook his head.

"Are *you* worried?"

"I don't think so . . . "

"That's hardly reassuring."

"Have you had any visitors?" Brian asked, hoping he wasn't overstepping.

"Not really. I haven't long moved in myself so have barely had time to tell people my new address."

"So, this guy under investigation hasn't visited you?" Brian said.

Yuki frowned, then scowled. "What do you think? Matter of fact, the only guy I keep seeing around here is you."

Brian's face flushed. "What are you saying? This has nothing to do with me."

"Brian, you need to calm down, or you run the risk of having another episode."

Brian breathed deep. "I'm sorry it's just, I'm not used to all these questions, first the PI, now you. Makes me feel like I'm guilty of something, but I swear to you, I've done nothing wrong—I've only ever done what felt right. What *was* right."

Yuki leant in close, spoke low. "I didn't mean to upset you, darling. I'm only trying to understand what's going on here." She cocked her head to the side. "But you see the PI again and you tell me, okay?"

Was Yuki concerned or scared? Was she somehow in on things? And what in the blue fuck were *things* anyway? Brian clenched his fists. That bloody PI had frazzled his mind. Had the bastard fucked with his brain? When Ted had conked Brian with his skull, had he caused some kind of brain damage? Was that why Brian had had a panic attack? He needed to get away from Yuki and from the apartments before he did or said something dumb.

"We should both get going," Brian said. "You have yoga and I have to . . . "

"Go to the doctors?"

"Perhaps."

"Panic attacks can be serious," Yuki said. "My mother was like you to begin with, but then she was forced into action."

"It's probably just cos I was . . . "

"Because you were what?"

Brian couldn't finish. No way was he telling her what had actually happened. "Last night was rough, is all."

"It takes more than whiskey to cause a panic attack, Brian."

A headbutt *was* more than whiskey.

Yuki toyed with her ponytail. "Take control of your health before your health takes control of you."

"I'll think about it."

"You better." Yuki blew Brian a kiss before getting in her car.

Soon Brian was on the road, but he couldn't stop thinking about the PI's words: D.T.A, D.T.A, D.T fucking A.

━◆━

When Brian entered the café, Lexie already had his cup of coffee upon the counter. She shot Brian a glowing smile and for a moment all his worries evaporated.

"It's good to see you, mister," she said, which charmed Brian until he remembered *Her* had called him mister, too, leaving him uneasy.

Brian gestured to the coffee. "So, either you've gained some special powers since I last saw you or—"

"Oh, I noticed you up the road a few minutes ago. I figured there was a ninety-percent chance you were heading here and what do you know, the odds were in my favour."

"Damn. Am I that predictable?"

"Dependable. You're dependable."

Brian liked that. He hadn't met many people who viewed him that way. The café was mostly empty, as was often the case, and Lexie slipped away from the counter and the two of them settled at a table near the door.

Lexie reached across the table for Brian and their hands found each other for a moment, but Brian didn't think it right to let them linger so reached back for his mug and drank.

"Tell me what's wrong," Lexie said.

He hadn't said anything was awry. Hadn't pre-warned her or texted ahead to let her know he needed to talk, and yet she'd known. So tell her he did. And unlike with Yuki he held nothing back.

After Brian was done, there was a lengthy silence as Lexie considered the facts.

When she was ready to talk, her eyes widened. "Obviously you have to go back."

"To the house?"

Lexie giggled and Brian couldn't help but grin. Her delight was infectious.

"Of course, to the house," she said. "Where else?"

"But why?"

"Why? Okay, now I can't tell if you're fucking with me or not . . . "

"I'm not."

She giggled again. "Brian! Come on now, you have to go back and find out what's inside."

"But isn't that kind of dangerous?"

"Isn't all fun fraught with an element of danger?"

Brian didn't know about that and besides, the way the PI had spoken about the guy who owned the near derelict house, he was highly dangerous.

"Aren't you even a little curious about what's inside?" Lexie asked.

She'd got him there. Of course he was.

"See!" Lexie said. "I knew it. Here's a thought, what if the PI isn't a PI, what if he's in on it?"

"In on *what?*"

"That's why you have to check the house. To find out."

"I'm not so sure about that. And besides, the PI and the other guy, they couldn't be more different. You've got one who lives in luxury, another who I'd wager can barely afford to pay the electricity bill. I honestly can't imagine them working together."

"Which is why it's the perfect cover. Could be a ruse."

"I guess it's possible, but it seems far-fetched."

"The so-called PI only made himself known when you went to enter the house. You think that was just a case of timing? A coincidence?"

"I suppose that is what I thought . . . "

"Only one way to know for certain."

"Say that you're right, won't it be even harder to return? If the two of them are working together, the PI will have tipped the guy off. There's no way I'm getting inside undetected. But if they're not working together, then it's as the PI says it is."

"Hmm . . . but he didn't say much, did he? You know what you have to do, Brian."

Whilst Brian was settling up with Lexie, he remembered the 'Get Out' note.

"So, there was one more thing," he said.

"Of course."

"I got this note through my door, not long after moving in."

"Oh?"

"It said 'Get Out'."

"Ah," Lexie said, as if that explained everything, which was similar to how the PI had been—so blasé, as if it was how all residents were welcomed.

"What do you think that was all about?"

Lexie's phone lit up and she picked it up on autopilot, mouthed 'sorry' when she realised her faux pas.

"Should I be worried?" Brian asked.

Brian felt a hand brush his shoulder. He turned around to see the woman from the previous day, the one in the vinyl trousers, only now she was wearing skinny cut jeans and a floral blouse. "Are you quite finished?" she said, as friendly as a kick in the balls.

"We were just having a conver—"

"Is this a fucking social club or a café?"

"Well, it's a—" Brian began.

"Hey," Lexie said. "He's a customer, don't be so rude. He's as much right to be here as you have."

She snorted. "Does he fuck? Coming around here and asking questions when he should just mind his own business."

"I was just—" Brian said, but she was quick to cut him off.

"Stay in your fucking lane! And don't ask any more questions."

"Karen," Lexie said. "I'm going to have to ask you to leave if you don't cool it."

"Yeah, well, good luck with that one." Karen grunted, pointing a finger at Lexie then Brian. "I want you twos to know, that I'm leaving, but not because you told me to because I have a right to be here, but because I'm choosing to leave. I'm leaving as a . . . as an . . . individual." She backed towards the door, pushing it open with her arse. She pointed her fingers towards her eyes and then to Brian. "I'm watching you, mate. I'm fucking watching you."

Once Karen was gone, Lexie handed Brian his change and receipt. "Don't worry about her and don't take it personally, she's like that to most people," she said. "She's an old busybody who needs to take up a hobby and cut back on the gin. Now about that old house, if you want, I could tag along. I'll be your Robin, what do you say?"

"My Robin?"

"As in Batman and Robin . . . "

"Oh? No, I don't think that's a good idea—"

"Because?"

What could Brian say to that? *Because I've already put Yuki in danger and don't want to hurt another person I . . .* Brian ran a hand through his hair.

"I just want to do this on my own."

Lexie looked down for a moment. Soon she was smiling again. "Well then, I'll be seeing you, mister. You know what you have to do. Now go be a hero."

SIXTEEN

SEEING LEXIE WAS supposed to bring clarity, but Brian's head was more frazzled than ever, especially after Karen had bumbled her way into his business. And what was with Lexie telling him to be a hero? What wasn't she telling him? What the hell did she think was inside that old house? Brian wanted to return to the house, like *really badly*, and he trusted Lexie, had already come to think of her as a friend, but the PI was a big guy, an intimidating guy, a guy who had warned Brian to stay the fuck away. Those hadn't been his exact words, but they might as well have been. And old Ted packed a punch. Not just with his words but his fists. Brian knew that first-hand and wasn't eager to experience anything like that again. Before doing anything rash, Brian wanted to learn more about the house which meant conducting a little research. But not on his own devices—he had no desire to leave a digital footprint. Which was how he found himself in the local library, hunched over a faded cream computer running an operating system several versions out-of-date.

As far as Brian could tell it was just him and the librarian in the building, an old lady called Margaret who'd told him four times to let her know if he needed help with anything. At first Brian thought Margaret was keeping tabs on him, but he'd soon settled, telling himself she was likely just lonely or suffering from a memory problem.

He began with Google Maps, tracing the journey from his apartment to the street with the old house. He hadn't been able to use street view for all of the route—where his apartment block now lay, stood rows of council houses, each as ugly and inhospitable as the next. The field with the tall grass was also absent from street view's coverage, though locating the rundown place proved easy enough. Even in the daylight it looked uninviting—poison ivy snaking up the front of the building, cautioning all who approached. There was no sign of the old banger on either the driveway or down the road which disappointed Brian who'd been hoping to identify the exact make and model. Still, he had the street name and house number which was more than enough to fuel further search enquiries. He got optimistic at first, putting just the address into Google which merely returned the very map he'd been looking at, in addition to estate agent listings, and the estimated market value for all properties on that street. Nothing of interest. Brian would have to get creative. He kept the street name, omitting the house number, as he trial-and-errored various terms such as 'crime', 'murder', 'tragedy', 'accident', 'missing', and even 'red robe'. Nothing relevant landed.

Brian punched the table, shaking the mouse and keyboard. "God damn it!"

He'd been a fool about the entire thing. How naïve for him to think he was just gonna stumble upon *what* exactly? Some wicked secret the town harboured? Easy answers? This wasn't some dumb film or make-believe story—this was real life for fuck's sake. He'd been so intoxicated by *Her*, letting his imagination run wild in more ways than one.

"That's enough."

Brian turned around, smelling the thick wave of masculine cologne. Ted stood behind him, a firm hand on Brian's shoulder. "You're coming with me. Don't make a scene."

Brian wanted to make a scene. To run around the library, tearing books off of the shelves until Ted got the hell away. He wanted to tell the guy to fuck off. To tell him enough was enough. To shout, 'D.T.A! D.T.A is right. I don't trust anyone and that includes you.' But Ted towered above him and everything from 'head to toe' screamed 'don't fuck with me'. Plus, Brian knew he'd done wrong, had been caught in the act, doing the only thing the PI had insisted he did not do.

Brian closed the browser, stood up, and followed Ted out the door.

SEVENTEEN

THEY WALKED IN silence, past the town proper, and down some side streets until they arrived at Ted's car. The BMW beamed, appearing shinier and fancier in the daylight. Brian went to say as much, to break the quiet and ease the tension, but Ted got there first.

"You stupid bastard!" he screamed so loudly Brian's shoulders involuntarily quaked back in surprise. "What did I tell you?"

"About what?"

"Don't play dumb with me, kid. Not after the morning I've had. If you knew half the things I know, you would *not* be fucking around like this."

"I don't understand."

"And it's better that way. Trust me, I fucking know. Now get in the car."

Brian looked in the car, then back to Ted. "I'm not getting in the—"

"Yes, you are. And don't expect me to be as patient as I was last night. You get in the car in ten seconds or you're riding in the boot again. Now which is it?"

"Wait." Brian held up his hands in surrender. "I'm listening, I'm cooperating, I'll do what you say."

Ted nodded. "About the smartest thing I've heard you say since we met. Now get in."

"My car's just a few streets away. Parked in the pay and display, a couple of minutes from here."

"That's a nice story. Now . . . " Ted gestured to the BMW.

"Please," Brian said. "I've got less than an hour on the car parking and I don't want to get another fine."

"Oh my god," Ted said, this time more exasperated than angry. "Why are you so pathetic?"

"I don't think it's unreasonable to not want to pay a fine for—"

"Here's the deal, I'll drop you at your car, and you'll follow me to the letter. I want you driving at the same pace and taking the same turns. No funny business. You got it?"

"Where exactly are we—"

"Brian, you're a few words away from laying on your back. You hear what I'm saying?"

"I hear you."

"Good. Now if you deviate, if you stop off for petrol, if you so much as let a single vehicle get between your car and mine, there will be severe consequences." Ted cleared his throat. "I'll beat you so badly you won't be able to lie down properly for the next month. Are we crystal?"

Private investigators sure handled things more directly than the regular police. Or at least differently than how Brian imagined they went about things, seeing as he'd had limited interactions with the law.

They got in the car. Metallica kicked in, a track from one of their earlier albums that Brian couldn't place. The car engine thundered up, and they raced down the street, towards the roundabout and A-road out of town.

"The car park's back—"

"I know where the car park is, son."

Brian swallowed. He didn't want to argue with the PI, especially given his current temperament, but Brian was fairly sure they'd driven further than even the most circuitous of long way rounds. By the time they got to the B-roads, surrounded by tall trees that made mid-morning look closer to early evening, Brian had clued into what was going on.

"We're not going to the car park, are we?"

The PI sniggered, which was the nearest he'd come to a smile all day.

It was at that point Brian figured out the name of the Metallica track, 'Escape'—too cruel given the circumstances.

"I can't believe you tricked me," Brian said.

"And I can't believe you were dumb enough to carry out your own investigation . . . in broad daylight . . . on a public computer. Bloody hell. I'm beginning to think your stupidity knows no bounds."

"I thought I was being smart."

"Yeah? I can't wait to hear the flawed logic on this one."

"It just didn't seem wise to use my own computer, is all."

"You shouldn't have been looking into this in the first place. What did I tell you?"

Brian shrugged. "It's not a crime to look into things. To do a little research. Isn't that your job?"

"Yes, son, that's *my* job. It isn't a crime to wire a house for electricity either but if something goes wrong, you're gonna get hurt."

Brian didn't know much about any of that, though his gut told him the analogy was tenuous.

"I told you not to go digging around," Ted said softly. "To leave things to me. Trust me, this is a situation where ignorance very much *is* bliss. Things might be too late for me, but they're not for you . . . at least, they weren't."

Brian stewed for a moment, then sighed. "I just wish you'd be more direct with me, to let me in on things."

"I'm telling you as much as I can. Probably a little more. Believe it or not, I'm doing this for your own good."

"Sounds like the kind of thing a parent would tell a kid when they don't have a real reason for some arbitrary rule they magicked up."

"Do you have a kid?" Ted's spit spattered the steering wheel. "No, you don't. You don't know what you're talking about, so shut the fuck up."

Brian placed his hands in his lap and said nothing. They rode the rest of the journey in silence.

⌐◥◣⌐

When they arrived at Ted's manor house, an Alsatian ran around from the back of the house and charged straight at them. Brian raised his fists in defence but soon lowered them when Ted began petting the dog and telling her what a good girl she was.

After Ted was done fussing, he side-eyed Brian: "Never try to fight Marcy."

Brian nodded and the two of them made their way inside the house, taking their shoes off in the entrance, and heading to the kitchen.

118

"Drink?" Ted asked.

Brian pulled his phone from his pocket, checking the time. "A little early, don't you—"

"I'm not talking about alcohol." He tapped the coffee maker on the worktop. "Want a cup?"

Ted didn't wait for an answer, taking two cups from the wall-mounted rack.

"Is the coffee cold?"

Ted scoffed. He took the three-quarters full jug from the maker and poured coffee into a mug, the steam from the cup answering Brian's question.

"Milk and sugar?"

"Just milk," Brian said, then almost as quickly and far too loudly: "Wait!"

So Ted did.

Brian stood there, trying to recall exactly what Yuki had ordered. There'd been vanilla, cream, and sugar, but he couldn't recall the quantities.

"Well?" Ted said.

"Got any vanilla?"

"Fucking hell, kid. This isn't a café. Milk and sugar? Yes or no?"

"Yes."

Ted added milk. Heaped in a spoonful of sugar. "How many?"

"A lot."

"A number please."

Brian hadn't seen how many sugars Yuki had taken but remembered something about high metabolism. "I dunno, maybe six?"

"Kid, if I put six sugars in your coffee, you're going to be bouncing off the ceiling."

"You'll shoot me?"

119

"What in the hell are you talking about? No one's shooting anybody. What I'm saying is, you'll be high as a kite."

Brian looked up at the ceiling, taking in the light fixture and smoke alarm.

"You're getting two sugars." Ted finished the drinks and passed Brian his coffee. "Now, to the sitting room."

They took to the same seats they had the previous evening, though this time there was no roaring fire and Marcy settled at her master's feet.

"She's a cute—"

"You're not a dog person and you don't have to pretend to be."

Ted took his cigarettes from his pocket. After lighting up he flung them towards the coffee table much as he had the other day. They landed in the centre, next to a framed photo of a young boy wearing a smart shirt and waistcoat. The boy's smile was wide, and he had a strong resemblance to Ted. Brian went to ask if he was Ted's son when he remembered how much Ted had flipped out when Brian had mentioned parents and kids on their way to the manor house. Brian kept quiet.

"Let's get down to business, you're probably wondering why you're here," Ted said.

"You said get in the car and then—"

"Not *how* but why. Though, I reckon you knew that. I'll tell you this, you've picked the wrong day to be a smart arse, the sooner you drop this . . . this . . . well, whatever the fuck this is, the better."

Brian drank his coffee, almost choking on the taste. It was more like a dessert with all that sugar.

But if it worked for *Her,* he could make it work for him.

"Looking into things on a public computer . . . For fuck's sake, man."

"You already said."

"Yeah? Well it bears repeating. That level of stupidity is—"

"Pretty convenient you happened to be walking by at the exact moment I was in the library, don't you think?"

"No, Brian, I don't think it was *convenient.* I was tracking you."

Brian had never met someone who so flagrantly spied on others. Did the man have no shame?

"Am I a person of interest?" Brian asked. "I thought you said—"

"You're a pain in the arse, is what you are. There's never been anyone quite like you who's—oi, stop smiling, son, it's not a compliment. Anyway, to get to the point, there's been a development. A lead that might well put an end to this entire thing. But I've got to tread carefully. One wrong move and this entire investigation goes to shit. Which is why I want you here."

"To help?"

"To stay out of the way."

"I don't think—"

"There's a big bedroom with a bathroom opposite on the first floor. I reckon you'll be comfortable there. Plenty of things to keep you occupied, including a large television with a Blu-ray player and all sorts of subscriptions: Netflix, Amazon, Now TV, and even some lesser-known services. I'll hook up a games console, too."

Brian scratched his head. "You want me to be your new roommate?"

"Christ no. But I do want you to stay here for a few days."

"So I don't *interfere* with things?"

"Partly that, partly for your own safety."

"And what about *Her?* What about Yuki's safety? If something's going to happen at Pelagic Court then I need to be there, to protect her, to save her." Brian stood up. "We should get Yuki now."

"Sit your arse back down and relax. Yuki will be fine."

"No, I will not sit down." Brian ran his hands through his thin hair. "Exactly what the fuck are you doing?

"Working my case."

"No shit. I'm talking about me being here. You . . . you can't do this." Brian made a fist, shook it at Ted. "You can't fucking do this. I'm going to the police."

"Brian . . . "

"I'll tell Yuki."

Ted sighed, then pursed his lips. He took a deep breath. "I understand you may have some reservations about—"

"Reservations? *You think?*"

"Let me finish, okay? I get it, I'm asking a lot. But there's so much on the line. Give me a week. Stay here, let me work my—"

"A week? Out of the question." Brian started pacing. "I'll give you twenty-four hours."

"That's hardly enough time. You realise this is seriously fucking dangerous, right? We're talking life and death. Your life. Yuki's life."

THEY'RE WATCHING

"Twenty-four hours or you can take me back to my car."

Ted looked at his hands. "Three days. It won't be easy and I'll have to speed things up and take some chances—but if you give me three days, I'll make it work. And if I can't, you get to go home anyway. How's that?"

"How's *that?* It's a bag of shit, is how it is."

Ted glared.

"Watch your mouth, son. Three days."

"No way. I said I'd give you twenty-four hours, though the more I think about it, the stupider it seems. Why the hell should I stay here? I'm not sitting on my arse with Yuki in danger. She could be dead in three days. Give me some reassurances, some information, some promises that things will be okay."

Ted raised an eyebrow. "Do I strike you as the type of person who goes around making promises? Fact of the matter is this, I have a plan. A good plan. A plan that's going to get her out and to safety, just as I've done for you here. With only three days, I'll have to put it into action a little sooner than anticipated, but I'll make it work. In many ways I'm doing you a favour seeing as—"

"Yeah, yeah, it really felt like a fucking favour when you forced me to leave my car. Not everyone has money like you. I may not be amongst the worst off, but I'm certainly not rich. A few hundred quid out of pocket is gonna sting."

"I'll take care of it."

"I don't want your money."

"Nobody said anything about money."

"Then how—"

"Like I said, I'll take care of it. Matter of fact, it's already taken care of."

"Just like that?"

"Just. Like. That."

"I guess you know all the right people in this town?"

"I know the right people, the wrong people, the somewhere-in-between people."

"What kind of a thing to say is that?"

"It's an honest thing, Brian. Something you could learn from. Put it like this, you want me on your side."

Brian squirmed in his seat. Ted smoked.

"The thing about Yuki—" Brian started.

"Is that neither of us really know her," Ted finished.

"That's bullshit."

"Yeah? Then tell me what you know."

Brian's brain was scrambled, the PI playing tricks on him, trying to catch him out and force him to say something he'd later regret. He refused to play along.

"That's what I thought," Ted said. "I know you care for her and I know you're a good guy, deep down, but you've got to cool off and let me handle things. I will do what I can for Yuki, but you'd be wise to remember that neither of us know the full extent of her involvement. Now I'm not saying she *is* involved, I'm just saying her motivations and such aren't clear."

"She's got an interview at The Dolori Academy for goodness' sake. Do you really think they'd consider someone with anything less than a spotless record? Have you any idea of the lengths they'll go to vet someone?"

THEY'RE WATCHING

Ted stretched back in his chair, patted his legs, and Marcy leapt up to join him. "Honestly, I've no idea what you're talking about."

"The Dolori Academy. It's the most prestigious dance academy in the world. Only three locations, one in Italy, Germany, and England." Brian said it as if it was so obvious, as if *everyone* knew the good old Dolori, as if he hadn't learnt about it from Yuki mere hours ago.

"Well, I'm glad you take such a keen interest in dance. But an interview at some academy, or anywhere for that matter, doesn't mean I'm gonna take shortcuts or give someone a free pass. I do my job properly."

"She's done nothing wrong."

"I appreciate your loyalty to her and I'm sure she does, too. But if you make one wrong move, it not only jeopardises your life and mine, but it could put hers at risk."

"I would never do that."

"Good, then you'll stay here. Play some video games, watch a few films—have yourself a nice little holiday."

"No."

"Three days. Two nights."

"I said, no *already*!"

"No isn't an option." Ted scratched his trunk of a neck. "And besides, what else do you have to do?"

Brian thought about the hole in the wall but even he wasn't stupid enough to mention it to Ted. "I need to protect Yuki."

"Staying here is how you protect her."

Brian snapped his fingers. "I've got it. Let me work with you."

"I don't need a sidekick. And besides, my status comes with certain liberties, something you don't have. I can get closer to things—dangerous things—but you, you'd be a liability, son."

Brian finished his coffee, put his head in his hands as he considered the hopelessness of the situation.

"Come on now, I'll show you to your room."

EIGHTEEN

I
T WAS A pleasant enough room, fancier than any place Brian had ever lived or even stayed in, and Ted had given him not one but two games consoles. That piece-of-shit PI was trying to buy Brian off with amenities and electronics. The joke was, it almost worked. Though the more Brian considered his reality, the sicker he became. Trapped in a single room for so long could get claustrophobic, not to mention he'd need food and fresh air. He'd said as much to Ted, who'd reassured him he was no prisoner and could roam the house and grounds as often as he liked. Brian was happy to hear he wasn't being kept captive but given Ted wasn't allowing Brian to go home, he called bullshit on it. Added to which, when Brian had asked if he could nip into town Ted had laughed, saying: "That I would not try." Brian had asked follow-up questions to clarify whether it was some sort of threat or merely a statement of fact because of the distance from the manor house to the town centre but Ted had lost his temper, shouting obscenities and punching a damn wall. Shortly after Ted had left the house, leaving Brian cross-legged on the centre of the plush bed, considering his options.

Brian reached for his smartphone, dropping a text to Helen: *Out of town for a bit. Call you in three days. Xx*

A little insurance policy in case Ted tried any funny business. It wasn't perfect, seeing as he didn't know where the fuck he was, but it was better than nothing. After sending the text message he turned off his phone. He didn't have his charger and wanted to conserve the battery. Plus he didn't want notifications going off and Ted taking an interest in his business. He'd pried enough.

There was an original Xbox and a PS3, with a handful of games for both. *Dead Space 2* caught Brian's eye. He turned on the TV and loaded a recent save file of a game in progress. After a few hours, Brian was running low on ammunition and health, so decided to save the game and stop playing. *See how you like that, Teddy boy!* As if in agreement, or perhaps disapproval, Brian's stomach rumbled.

He headed downstairs and into the kitchen where he began opening cabinets at random, hunting for a plate. Brian soon found the fine china cabinet. Staying in style meant dining in style, even if he was only making a sandwich. Ted's food supplies did not disappoint, in the cupboard lay a loaf of wholemeal bread that looked fancy without being pretentious, whilst in the fridge sat a fresh packet of honey roast ham, alongside naturally smoked cheddar cheese, chopped lettuce, and one of the reddest tomatoes Brian had ever seen. He built a sandwich, finishing the piece with a drizzle of spicy brown mustard.

He sat at the counter and ate, relishing every bite. His phone rested next to the plate. Periodically Brian reached for it as he contemplated turning it on and calling Yuki, but each time he went to power up the device he'd stall, remembering Ted's words: *her motivations and such aren't clear*. But Yuki couldn't be involved with the bearded man, right?

What if she was?

What if this was some weird game she liked to play, and Brian was a minor part of it? Maybe this was how she got her kicks, knowing the bearded man was watching her, throwing rocks at her window, tracking her movements. *And now there's this other plaything, a man called Brian, who watches me dance every night.*

Did Yuki know he was watching her, too?

Brian shook the thoughts away, embarrassed that in even thinking such things he was insulting *Her*, debasing the divine. Ted was trying to confuse Brian, planting seeds into his mind, playing tricks with his imagination to question his very loyalty to *Her*. D.T.A. Don't trust anyone. For Brian, that ultimately meant don't trust Ted. If there was a game, it was likelier it was Ted's. Some sick mind-fuck—perhaps a power play of sorts? Ted seemed the type who might be into that. Everything's all nice and squeaky clean at the house, but outside, in secret, he got his rocks off watching people. Ted said he'd been watching *Her* and the bearded man for a while. Ted bold-faced admitted he had been watching Brian as well.

Maybe Ted and the bearded man were co-conspirators, watching *Her* together.

And what did they do whilst they watched? Was there anything they didn't do? Were they both involved? Did they film it? Film each other as they—

Brian shook his head, was getting carried away, his thoughts, his fantasies—was that what they were?—swimming into overdrive. This all made little sense, but then wasn't that what Ted wanted everyone to believe—how could he be the pervert in this complete mess—how could he be the ultimate perpetrator? He was the private investigator. The very man working the case. Whatever 'the case' even was.

It was almost the perfect alibi.

Brian left the dirty plates and utensils in the sink.

Trying to remember where the main bathroom was, Brian tried a door in the hall that opened to a training room. There were a couple of dumbbells on the floor next to a weight bench, and in the corner lay a martial arts dummy covered with a ratty sheet. For a second Brian thought the sheet moved. He really didn't need to be in that room any longer, so closed the door behind him.

In the bathroom, Brian found a large towel under the sink and an unopened bar of soap. He preferred body wash, but this would do. The shower was one of those glassed in units with the drain in the centre. He set the water temperature just right and took a long and steamy shower—exactly what he needed to clear his mind and relax his nerves.

Whilst drying off, he realised there was one thing Ted hadn't thought of for Brian's brief holiday away from the apartment. Brian wrapped the towel around his waist and returned to the room he was staying in. There was plenty of clean underwear in the chest of drawers, and trousers and shirts in the wardrobe, but none of it would fit Brian properly. Ted was more or less Brian's height, but around two stone heavier.

THEY'RE WATCHING

There was no way Brian was wearing those baggy trousers, even if he was simply lounging around the house. Should he ring Ted and demand he pick up some new clothes? Brian reached for his wallet, retrieving the card Ted had given him earlier—he stared at the number like it might give him a sign or at least a new pair of trousers. Fuck it, he'd wear the clothes he'd had on earlier—a simple reminder that Ted was just another bastard—a bastard who didn't give a shit about anything other than his precious investigation.

Back in the bathroom, Brian found a new can of deodorant under the sink, as well as a sealed toothbrush and tube of toothpaste. Whilst brushing his teeth, the reality of the situation dawned on him. Every second he stayed in the house, two things were happening. One, Ted was practically holding him against his wishes, and two, assuming Ted was right, Yuki was in grave danger. This investigation concerned Brian, and yet Ted refused to share much of the details. That wasn't fair. Brian had a right to know, especially if his or Yuki's life was at risk.

What if Ted had stirred up so much trouble with all his snooping that they—whoever *the fuck* they were—knew of Ted's movements?

What if *they* were watching him? Tracking him?

That being the case, they'd surely know Brian was here, in the manor house.

Oh fuck!

Ted might have unwittingly kicked up one shit-fuck of a hornet's nest. A good private investigator would know how to cover their tracks, but whether Ted was a *good* PI Brian could not say. Matter of fact, the only thing proving he was a PI—let alone a decent one—was Ted's word and the card he'd handed Brian.

Brian got dressed into his now crumpled clothes, which was what he deserved for scattering them across the bathroom floor.

He paced into the bedroom. Brian hadn't closed one of the drawers properly, a pair of Ted's grey briefs jutted out the side. The last thing Brian wanted was for Ted to think he'd been going through his underwear. He pulled the drawer out, folding the briefs neatly. But that didn't look right either. They were too tidy. The rest of the underwear had been haphazardly stuffed into the drawer. *Fuck's sake, Ted, I hope you handle your business better than your clothes.* Brian shuffled the underwear as if a deck of cards, which was when he discovered the Polaroids sandwiched in the middle. He lay the photographs on the top of the chest of drawers.

#1 The front of Pelagic Court. Nobody about. Notes of purple in the sky. Brian's Ford Focus parked up.
#2 A close-up of a window.
#3 A second window close-up. Yuki stared out, hair wrapped in a lilac towel, black night robe on.
#4 Yuki standing outside Dylan & Son supermarket. Camera facing. Carrier bag in her left hand. Bottle of water in her right, raised to her lips.
#5 A park playground. Empty save for a woman in the distance, sitting on a swing. Long hair swaying in the breeze.
#6 The ocean at dawn. A woman in rainbow yoga pants bent over, buttocks towards the camera, hands in the sand, in some sort of yoga pose.

THEY'RE WATCHING

What in the hell was going on here? Ted had said he was investigating, asking questions, making enquiries, but this right here was pure voyeurism. He'd said the guy with the beard was a person of interest, not Yuki. She'd been what? Just someone he needed to follow up with, to possibly protect. Brian's stomach gurgled. His bowels loosened. He rushed to the bathroom.

✒◄►

After Brian had finished arse and mouth puking, he made his way into the sitting room and sat in the recliner—staring into space. Was there an innocent explanation to those photographs or was the most dangerous threat of all to Yuki, Ted himself? Those snaps were salacious, especially that final shot on the beach, the lens practically ogling her arse. And what of the shot in her night robe? Even the way she held the water bottle to her mouth had an element of eroticism to it.

Ted was a fucking creep.

Unless . . . No, it couldn't be, but Brian supposed there was the slim possibility, but no he was a good person, but even so what if, what if it was Brian who was adding the damn near pornographic bent to the photographs? What if it was all in his mind? What if Brian was the sick one?

"Yeah, right. This is a literal wank bank!" Brian screamed and Marcy scurried over. "No, fuck off, Marcy, I'm trying to think." And as if well-versed in English, she exited towards the dining room.

Brian rapped his fingernails against the recliner's arm. They were just photographs. He needed to stop

133

assuming things, making wild leaps with no evidence. This was why Ted was the investigator and Brian wasn't, because he was too heavily influenced by his heart and not his mind. He couldn't divorce emotion and feelings from reality and facts.

Brian wanted to call Yuki, to hear her voice, to *know* she was okay. But he didn't want to do anything rash, didn't want to risk bringing more harm to her or himself or even Ted. He needed to look out for the three of them. *Ugh*, was that how it was now? Three of them? Brian clenched his fists. He didn't like the thought of that one bit.

Did Ted being on the case mean the local police had either exhausted their evidence or were no longer interested in the leads?

Could it be worse? Were they somehow involved? Complicit?

The net of who *They* were was forever widening.

Too many questions and yet they kept on coming, because the truth was, Brian knew almost fuck all. He could count the points on one hand, which was nowhere near good enough. There were plenty of reasons to be wary of Ted. And yet he'd put Brian up in a well kitted-out room and given him permission to explore the entire house—to take and use whatever he needed. He hadn't taken his wallet or phone or anything like that. The PI's hospitality was generous and without too many reservations other than the whole 'don't leave the house' thing.

Brian wouldn't call *Her*.

Couldn't risk it.

What if Ted was legit?

THEY'RE WATCHING

Even if everything Ted was and wasn't telling Brian was true, even if those photos were innocent, it angered Brian that he wasn't the one getting *Her* out of danger. How dare Ted, some rich-ass private investigator, take that privilege—that absolute *honour*—away from Brian.

Yuki *needed* Brian. And he needed *Her*. And not after waiting it out for three fucking days. This was an emergency, god damn it.

Brian sat bolt upright. Absolute clarity washing over him for the first time since entering the manor house. He had to be the one to get *Her* out of danger and into safety.

Into his loving arms.

Brian stood up, ready to act. As soon as the opportunity presented itself, he'd get away from the house and find *Her*. If he had to get his hands dirty, if he had to bleed, it would all be worth it for Yuki. For *Her* was energy, *Her* was life, *Her* was everything.

NINETEEN

FOR A FEW glorious seconds, Brian felt charged and elated—believing he could and would do anything. Then it dawned on him, he hadn't the slightest idea where Ted had gone or how long he'd be. Given Brian had pissed much of his time away playing *Dead Space* and a not insubstantial chunk fixing himself an elaborate sandwich he wasn't even sure how much time had passed.

What the hell is wrong with me?

Brian walked to the front-facing window. Ted's car still wasn't in the driveway and there was no sign of it further up the road either—not that the trees allowed him to see too far into the distance.

Brian felt the weight of his car keys in his pocket and silently cursed. If his car wasn't miles away things would be much easier. He supposed he could head out on foot—walking just deep enough into the woods that passing vehicles wouldn't detect him, but near enough the road he'd be afforded a decent amount of light. The sun would set in a few hours and whilst it hadn't taken Ted too long to drive the two of them back to the manor house, Brian wasn't keen on risking it. He'd seen enough horror films to know what could happen if you got lost in the woods after dark. If only

THEY'RE WATCHING

Uber operated in these parts, but alas, Brian was a long way from the city, and given Ted's connections, calling a local taxi was tantamount to Brian phoning Ted himself and letting him know he was planning on leaving. The speed at which Ted had summoned a taxi the other day had been eerily quick, especially given he lived out in the sticks. No, getting up early and slipping out tomorrow morning was the more sensible plan. When he was some distance from the house he could call an out-of-town private taxi to come pick him up.

But what if there is no tomorrow?

Brian latched onto the thought. Helen was always berating him for being too slow to act—putting things off and costing himself opportunities. This was one of those moments. If he didn't act quickly then shit would go wrong. But this wasn't a case of missing out on an interview or a date, this could prove fatal.

Brian rushed to the front door. Locked from the outside.

Fuck's sake, Ted!

So much for not being a prisoner. And talk about a bloody fire hazard.

D.T.A. Don't trust anyone.

Brian headed through the kitchen to the back door which was secured with three locks. Fortunately, this time, they were all accessible from inside. As soon as Brian began unlocking the door, Marcy trotted up behind him.

"You need some air too, huh?"

Marcy stared up at him with wide hopeful eyes. He opened the door and the dog raced outside. Brian stepped out onto the patio, smelt the cool, crisp air and freshly cut grass. He noted the edges around the patio, immaculately trimmed. There were two luxury deckchairs, arranged side by side, an ashtray next to one of them, overflowing with cigarette butts. Some butts were lipstick stained. The thought of Ted entertaining a female guest disgusted Brian. Did he take secret photos of them, too? He figured Ted for the old-school PI type, hanging out with prostitutes, drinking and smoking together, before they retired to the bedroom for sweaty, raunchy sex. Definitely not the kind of sex he and Yuki would eventually have.

Her would not just have sex.

Her would make love.

Her would transcend.

Brian smiled at the thought, though it quickly soured. He couldn't shift the image of Ted having clumsy, graceless sex—wheezing and grunting, an overabundance of sweat dripping from his greasy brow. Brian could practically smell it.

Ugh! Brian wanted to slap himself. He turned away from the deckchairs, scanning for a way out. The fence around the garden was wooden and appeared new. There was a gated door, and Brian could see the padlock, glaring in the sunlight. But looking for the key would take time, which made Brian uneasy. The fence stood around one and a half times taller than Brian. He wasn't in the best shape but reckoned he could scale it if he absolutely had to.

Brian checked his pockets: keys, phone, wallet—everything he needed.

Time to leave.

As soon as Brian stepped on the grass, ready to make a run for the fence, Marcy dashed over from the other side of the patio and started growling at him. Brian put his hands up, praying she wouldn't pounce.

She began to bark.

"Shh," Brian said, which only made her bark louder.

He lowered his head and ambled back inside. Last thing he needed was a barking dog alerting anyone nearby that a man was scaling the fence. It didn't look like anyone lived in the vicinity—didn't seem like there were any other houses for miles, just trees and woods—but with the way Brian's luck was going, Ted would have some weird security system that triggered a call to the police as soon as Brian climbed atop the fence—motion sensors or some shit like that. It was far-fetched and out-of-the-ordinary, but then so was fucking everything since moving to Pelagic Court. Brian re-locked all the doors and went back to sit on the recliner.

Where in the hell was Ted, anyway? He hadn't left so much as a note and whilst Brian supposed, as a grown-ass man, he didn't need other grown-ass men to leave him notes or check in with him, it was almost evening, and Ted was nowhere to be seen. Obviously, he was a busy guy, and maybe he was working more than one case, but that didn't help Brian with his present predicament. Not knowing when his captor would return made making a decision mighty difficult.

Helen was right. Brian was afraid of commitment.

Fuck this. He checked his pockets for the last time and walked over to the large front window. He tried the handle, almost laughing when it opened. The PI had made a point of locking the front door but hadn't bothered with the window leading to the driveway. *Not so fucking smart now, old Teddy boy!*

Still no sign of Ted's car.

Cool air breathed into the room. Brian lapped it up, filling his lungs. It wouldn't take any effort at all to climb through the window and stroll down the driveway towards freedom.

Then Ted's car careened around the corner and turned into the drive.

TWENTY

AT **FIRST**, Brian froze, caught in the middle of some great escape, as Ted parked up. But he soon came to his senses, shutting the window, and racing back to the recliner. *Just a regular man taking a regular breather, nothing strange going on at all.* Brian heard Ted enter the house, first fussing about removing his shoes in the hallway, and then heading to the kitchen. The aroma of smoky cumin, sweet liquorice, and garlic wafted up Brian's nostrils.

When Ted first entered the sitting room, Brian stopped himself from even looking in his direction, but quickly figured that made him look even guiltier. He stood to meet Ted, though meet was generous given the size difference.

Ted frowned. "What the hell are you up to?" Ted sounded more perplexed than angry.

Brian shrugged. "Just a normal guy doing normal guy things."

"You're a funny one."

"I went out in the back garden earlier, to get some fresh air."

"Good for you, kid."

"It was at first, but then Marcy started raising hell—barking so loudly it hurt my ears. I headed back

141

inside because I didn't want to disturb your neighbours."

"Neighbours? There's nobody around for fucking miles." Ted rubbed his hands on his face. "You know, come to think of it, it's a bit odd that Marcy was barking. You didn't touch her, did you? I told you not to fuck with her."

Brian put his hands up. "Not at all."

"Good," Ted said. "Though still, barking at you? It makes no damn sense. What were you doing? Trying to leave?"

"What? Are you crazy? You said three days not three hours!" Brian stepped back, shaking his hands—he hadn't put on a performance like this since GCSE Drama. "And besides, you're a private investigator, a position I've really come to respect—"

"Oh, you have now?"

"Uh-huh." Brian swallowed. "And because of that, because of my *respect*, when you say something I listen. And what you said was, what you said earlier, when we were . . . " Brian was losing it, adrenaline fumbling his words. "Well, point is, you said if I left then things might get dangerous, especially for Yuki and, well . . . like I said, I would never do anything to jeopardise her safety."

Ted nodded. "Glad to hear you've had a change of heart. Now stop pissing your pants and let's eat, yeah? I popped into The Raj on the way back—it's the best Indian restaurant in town. Got a little something for the both of us," Ted said, walking through to the kitchen.

Brian followed. He eyed the mountain of washing-up in the sink and instantly felt like an arsehole. "I hope you don't mind, but I made a sandwich for lunch."

"The ham's pretty tasty, huh?" Ted pulled takeaway containers from brown paper bags that rested on the kitchen surface.

"Sorry about the dishes. I'll take care of them now, if you—"

"Save it for later, I'm starving." Ted opened the backdoor. "Marcy? Marcy?" She sprinted towards Ted who gave her some fuss. "Happy as a pig in shit. Whatever startled her, she's fine now."

Once the food and plates were set, they settled at the dining room table, facing one another, tall bottles of Cobra beer to quench their thirst. Brian took a swig and felt more at ease, his failed escape attempt relegated to the back of his mind. Then he remembered the photos.

Ted prised the lids off of each of the containers, giving Brian a rundown. "I didn't know what you wanted, so I got us a mix of things. If you like it spicy, dig into the madras, the balti's more of a medium spice dish but has a kick to it, and the tikka masala might not pack much of a punch but it's the most flavoursome one I've ever tasted—unlike a lot of places I've been to over the years they don't over-sweeten it."

"Thanks," Brian said. The way Yuki had bent over in the downward dog pose at the beach, the camera lens ogling her, surely that was more than a routine investigation photo.

"Then you've got the pilau rice, the egg fried rice, and even some coconut rice. I haven't tried coconut before, but you strike me as the type who might be into it."

Brian kept quiet, wishing Ted would stop talking already. *It's curry, we're eating curry, okay? Leave it at that*! he wanted to say. Or, *leave the masturbatory stuff for your private photos, not food.* Only that wasn't right, he didn't want Ted masturbating over any of those photos. Matter of fact, Brian was tempted to march up to Ted's bedroom and destroy the bloody lot.

"As for side dishes, there's Bombay aloo, brinjal bhaji, saag paneer, and aloo gobi. And I probably don't have to explain to you that that big bastard over there's a naan bread, am I right?"

Brian nodded. *Shut the fuuuuuuuck up.*

"Well then, dig in."

The two ate. Ted greedily shovelling down food, Brian reluctantly edging pieces of potato into his mouth. Even the photograph of the window without Yuki standing in it might mean something. What if there were multiple copies of the Polaroids and Ted had shared a duplicate set with the bearded man? Was it so impossible the two of them were working together?

"Something bothering you, son?"

Brian chewed chicken. "I'm fine."

Ted cast a look that said he was calling bullshit, but he didn't follow-up. At least Ted had been right about the tikka masala, it was the freshest and richest Brian had ever experienced, the red less artificial than the ones he'd tried back in the Midlands, and the tomato more present. If it wasn't for those fucking photos, Brian would almost be enjoying himself.

Ted set his knife and fork down. "You didn't do anything stupid, did you?"

THEY'RE WATCHING

Brian swallowed his mouthful, looked at Ted, trying to figure out what he was getting at. Why the unprompted outburst?

Ted scratched his eyebrow. "You didn't call Yuki, or that sister of yours, or anyone else, right?"

"No, sir," Brian said, trying to feign respect, though in actuality, the way 'sir' squeaked out, it sounded as if he was taking the piss, making a joke at the PI's expense. It was a good job he didn't know about the text message to Helen.

Ted chowed down a chunk of potato. "Smart move, kid. Smart move. Don't want anyone getting hurt. Especially when there's little Gracie to think of."

Brian swallowed, willing his food to stay down. That sick fuck knew his niece's name and now what was he doing? Was he threatening Brian?

Brian switched gears, praying he didn't look as worried as he felt. "Did you make any headway today?"

"About the same as usual."

Brian waited for Ted to elaborate. When he didn't, Brian followed up. "How much progress do you usually—"

Ted slammed his fork onto the table. "If it's not too much to ask, I'd like to eat without giving you a rundown of my entire fucking day. To be honest, today was shit. I spent the entire time dealing with shitty things and piece-of-shit people—to top it all off, I've got shit all to show for my shitting efforts."

"I'm sorry. I was just trying to—"

"Well, don't."

Jesus Christ, Ted's moods had more back and forths than a game of tennis.

145

Brian polished off the saag paneer, the creamy cheese and soft spinach coupled with just the right amount of spice helped Brian feel better about irritating the PI, though no better about him mentioning Gracie or the damn Polaroids. As volatile as Ted was, Brian wanted to keep him talking, to figure out the guy's end game and just how legit he was. "You reckon they know you're watching them?"

Ted narrowed his eyes. "Why are you asking? You think I don't know what I'm doing?"

"No, no, I'm sure you do. I suppose I'm a little scared, that's all."

"Good. You should be scared. You should be shaking in fucking fear. It'll help keep you in check, will encourage you to do the right things and, more importantly, stop you from doing the wrong things."

Were the photos to keep Yuki in check? Blackmail if she stepped out of line.

Ted glugged back the rest of his beer. "There's always a chance I might get noticed. That's the problem, you rattle enough cages, eventually people pay attention. The key to this job is learning how to keep your distance. I take my time, gathering all the available intel on the target, before so much as approaching."

"The target? Are you saying what I think you're saying?"

"Not a clue seeing as I'm not a mind reader."

Brian leant closer. "Are you talking about killing?"

Ted snorted, pushed a hand through the air, forcing Brian to move back. "You silly son-of-a-bitch. Of course I'm not talking about killing."

"You said target, so I thought—"

"You didn't. You didn't *think*. We've been through this—you need to hold your thoughts back."

The PI hadn't a bloody clue how much Brian was holding back.

"Consider what you're about to say before you *actually* say it, kid."

Brian felt pressure fizzing in his head, but he wasn't embarrassed or anxious, he was downright insulted. The PI might be looking after him, giving him food and shelter, but all this condescension—calling Brian 'kid' and 'son' and acting like he was a moron. Brian was about to say as much when the PI started up again.

"With the target or person of interest, if you prefer, there's always a chance they're being blackmailed or bribed. When that kind of thing happens, not only does the individual lead me down the wrong path, but they often report back to whoever the hell was bribing them in the first place."

"Like a bent copper or something?"

"Unlikely to be the police. Not with this kind of thing. We're talking about the *actual* person of interest, someone who's got skin in the game, and something to hide. And when they get close, not only does the real game of cat and mouse begin but it becomes difficult to discern which is which. You follow what I'm saying?"

Brian's furrowed brow indicated he did not.

"What I'm saying is, information about me, perhaps even my photograph, could get into the wrong hands."

"You deal in photographs?" Brian said. "What does that even mean?"

"You mentioned photographs. Is that what you do? You take photographs of people?"

Ted combed his fingers through his hair. "Course I fucking do, but I think you're missing the point. What I'm saying is, if some bent bastard has *my* details or *my* photograph, the roles are reversed. Suddenly I'm the one being tracked—some undesirable's monitoring *my* movements, tapping *my* phone, perhaps even putting some electronic GPS device on my car."

"You're joking?"

"It's happened before. Several times, in fact."

"Fucking hell . . . "

Ted rose from his seat, started gathering up the leftovers, ready for the fridge. "That's enough talking. Give me a hand clearing the table and we'll get to the washing-up."

━━✦━━

Once they were done, the two men headed into the sitting room and slumped back in their respective sofa chairs with fresh bottles of Cobra. Some panel show hosted by Jimmy Carr played on the television, though neither Brian nor Ted paid it much attention as they rested their hands on their stomachs, nursing their food babies. At one point, Ted reached forward for the packet of Marlboros resting on the coffee table but ultimately decided against it and flopped back to a slouched position. Brian didn't drink much of the beer, wanting to keep his wits about him, but his eyelids were already starting to droop, the Indian having taken full effect, making them both drowsy. If Ted continued drinking it might loosen his tongue, allowing Brian to get to the bottom of the Polaroids. Ted had already mentioned he took photographs of people, which was a good start, but Brian needed more.

"Jolly good," Ted said.

"What is?" Brian squinted in Ted's direction, but Ted said nothing further so that was the end of that riveting exchange.

Numerous stares into empty space later Brian was on his feet. "I need to use the bathroom."

Ted grunted. Brian headed upstairs.

After he was done, Brian paused halfway down the stairs, catching Ted's reflection in the front window. He slouched back, just as still as he'd been when Brian had left. Brian wagered the PI hadn't so much as moved, had perhaps even fallen asleep. Brian checked his pockets for his keys, wallet, and phone. All three were on his person. If Ted was sleeping, this was a golden opportunity to escape. And if Ted caught Brian, he'd just tell him he was having a little stroll around the block to burn some calories after all that Indian food. He wasn't sure Ted would buy that bullshit but until he mustered up something better, he was sticking with it. Brian crept down the stairs as quietly as could be. When he reached the bottom, he hovered in the hallway, peering into the sitting room and listening closely. Ted's eyes were closed but Brian couldn't hear him snoring or breathing heavier, though from the television volume Brian was hard pushed to hear anything other than Jimmy Carr. Which was perfect—not Jimmy Carr's brand of comedy, obviously—but the fact the tv was so loud it drowned out all other sounds, meaning even if the door slammed shut, Ted would be none the wiser.

Ted's BMW keys were practically in front of him, sitting on the coffee table, calling Brian's name. Brian couldn't ignore that. The universe was telling him to go to Yuki, to be with *Her*. He reached the bottom of the stairs, tried the front door.

No such luck.

But that was okay, there were other ways out of the house, provided Marcy didn't show up and ruin everything with her yapping. He turned to the front window, hoping to hell that Ted hadn't locked it since returning home. Bracing himself, Brian turned the handle, nearly screaming with excitement when the window eased open and the night's fresh cold air kissed his cheek. A kiss that said, "We love you, Brian. We want you to succeed." The universe on his side once more. Brian concentrated on his heartbeat. He was so alive. So ready for this moment.

He peered over at Ted and his car keys. Would it be monumentally dumb to push his luck? To go for the keys and give himself an advantage over the PI? Ted hadn't stirred. Sleeping or dozing, though it had to be nearer to sleeping because the guy was oblivious to the wind whispering into the room and Brian practically standing over him like the lamest night terror.

Brian leant over to scoop up the car keys, accidentally jangling them. Ted snorted in his sleep, and Brian just about shit himself, dropping the keys and prompting further racket.

Brian froze, eyes on Ted. His snoring resumed. Brian looked at the keys. No way was he risking it again, had already damn near drained his luck. Better to go on foot.

THEY'RE WATCHING

He crept back to the window, crossing his fingers that Marcy wouldn't appear as he edged onto the ledge. He breathed a sigh of relief as his feet hit the floor.

Brian hummed Iron Maiden's 'The Trooper' in his head, which he always figured was the ultimate getaway tune. Before long he was racing up the driveway and singing aloud.

He reached the top of the driveway and screamed in pure ecstasy: "There's no turning back!"

Then he stepped from the driveway to the public road.

He was free.

Brian hurried down the road towards the town, keeping an eye out for landmarks that might help him pinpoint where he was, so he could call an out-of-town taxi. Thus far it was just trees, trees, and more trees, but sooner or later—and he really hoped sooner—there'd be something else, *anything* else. As Brian was walking, he realised he could just use his phone's maps application to locate his whereabouts. He got so giddy with excitement that he actually stopped in his tracks, pulling the phone from his pocket with gusto and powering it on.

Where the network name should have been was text reading 'no service'. No matter, sometimes these things took time. Brian resumed walking, half concentrating on the road ahead, half on the phone. He was just in a particularly rough patch with lousy reception and would soon get a bar or two. He hit recent calls and dialled a number at random, crossing his fingers it would jolt his service to life. When that didn't work, he powered off the phone, going for the old 'turn it off and on again' trick. It might have been off recently but 'turn it off and on' didn't necessarily have logic to it.

"Oi, stop running!"

Brian turned his head and saw Ted jogging down the road. For a big man, Ted was swift, easily catching up to Brian.

Oh Christ! It was now or never.

Brian stepped off the road and onto the grassy shoulder, next to the woodland, almost twisting his ankle in the soft ground. It hurt like hell but mercifully he didn't fall. The pain begged him to put his hands up, to throw in the towel there and then, but instead Brian kept moving towards the forest, the initial stabbing receding with each step. He'd be limping around tomorrow, but if he didn't keep moving, there might not be a tomorrow. He looked over his shoulder again, Ted much nearer now.

"STOP!" Ted said.

Brian tried to run, nearly tripping, he'd really done a number on his ankle.

"You want her to die?" the PI shouted.

That stopped Brian. He put his hands on his knees, he'd hardly moved and was already winded.

"You going to kill her?" Brian said, turning to face Ted.

Ted had stopped running. He stood still, fifteen or so feet behind Brian. Ted wasn't even breathing heavily.

"Is that the deal, huh? I stay here, or you kill Yuki?"

Ted shook his head. "Not me."

"Then who? Tell me, who the fuck will kill her? Are they going to kill me, too?"

152

"Look . . . I already told you."

"You've told me NOTHING!" Brian screamed, spittle flying from his mouth. "No. No, no, no. Fuck this. You can't keep me hostage."

Ted's mouth twisted into a grimace. "Listen, son, I get it. Really, I do. I'm just trying my best to keep anyone from dying. Yuki, you, me."

"I don't believe you." Brian stepped away from the trees.

"You have to believe me. Please."

"D.T.A. Ted. Isn't that what you always say . . . don't trust anyone?" Brian noticed Ted was holding something in his hand. "What's that?"

Ted flicked his wrist, extending the metal baton out to its full length. "It's for my safety."

"Safety?" Brian ran his hands through his thin sweaty hair.

"In case you attack me."

Brian took a deep breath. "Listen, man, I'm leaving and that's all there is to it—I'm leaving because you can't keep me here. Nothing more than that. I'm not going to hurt you, but I am going to leave. And once I'm out of here I'm going straight to Yuki. I won't tell her you kept me here, but I will tell her you're watching because that kind of thing isn't right, you know?"

Brian had sounded more confident than he felt, which almost made him grin, but he adjusted his expression, not wanting to piss off the big man.

"I'm just doing my job."

"Cut the bullshit, Ted. I know about the photos and I know why you took them. I've seen them all. You're a fucking predator, mate."

Brian started to turn, watching Ted the whole time. He had nothing to say about the Polaroids then. Confirmation in silence. Ted's game was up. For a split second, Brian believed Ted would actually let him leave, that he could just walk down the road until he got enough signal to find his location and call a taxi.

Then Ted flung the baton at Brian. It came at him so quickly he had no time to react.

The last thing Brian saw was the baton spinning wildly at his face.

TWENTY-ONE

WHEN BRIAN CAME TO, he was groggy as hell with what felt like the most monstrous hangover he'd ever endured. Bright white light flooded the room, stinging his half-open eyes. His throat dry, his bowels full, his head pulsating. For a moment Brian forgot where he was. Though *forgot* wasn't quite right, it was as if he had no recollection of anything—no place, no person, no event. Then he smelt it.

Shit.

Actual shit.

The stench of faeces hung heavily in the air. Brian tried moving his head, to locate the offending smell, but he was stiff as hell and it barely budged—each laboured movement produced stabbing pains in his neck.

He strained as hard as he could, felt something loosen in his gut.

Which was when he realised the smell was coming from him.

He'd soiled himself.

Brian gagged, his head moving involuntarily from the reflex, his eyes stinging and weeping from the ache.

Then everything went soft and fuzzy.

He awoke sometime later, his head now down. He saw his legs through blurred eyes, though his feet were out of range. He tried to move, as slowly as possible, and was met with more pain. He couldn't lift his head and couldn't move his arms.

He couldn't see his hands.

Was he paralysed?

Seemed unlikely. He *had* moved, though it had been stiff and agonising. He took a deep breath in, heard the joints click as he exhaled. He managed to move his head just enough to observe the intravenous pole next to him with a full bag of drugs. Brian still couldn't see his arms or hands, just the tops of his shoulders, but he wagered there was an IV slammed into his veins. If the bag was full of painkillers, they weren't working. Though the drugs might go some way to explaining why his vision hadn't fully returned.

Perhaps he'd had a stroke or something and was now in hospital. Brian concentrated, channelling all his energy towards retracing his steps, to uncovering lost memories, but everything remained a blur.

Where was the button to call a nurse? To let them know he was awake.

Brian opened his mouth to speak. A raspy croak sputtered out.

He coughed.

Noticed the chunks of vomit speckling his shirt.

Brian cleared his throat and tried again: "Help."

Christ, he sounded somewhere between a mouse and a boy. No way was he getting anyone's attention like that.

THEY'RE WATCHING

He closed his eyes, shielding them from the harsh intruding light.

Brian slumbered, and his dreams were of tornadoes chasing him through fields, though he could never get away. He ran and ran—the wind whipping up around him, flinging dirt and debris in every direction, darkening the sky. And screaming. Someone was screaming at him in the tornado.

A woman.

A woman screaming in the tornado.

Brian woke again, the woman's name on his lips.

Her.

He had to get to *Her.*

The dull throb in his head persisted, but he could move his neck better, and his eyesight was returning to normal. He looked around, struggling to remember, then it clicked.

Ted's house.

That's where he'd been.

Ted had kept him there. Pretty much against his god damn will and then what?

Brian scanned the room. This was no hospital. This was the bedroom he'd been staying in and yet it was different. The chest of drawers and desk remained but the television and games consoles were gone, making room for the IV and chair. He looked at the fluid bag, hanging from the pole, now empty. *Good.* Ted was taking care of him. Soon he'd return and change the bag, and Brian would ask questions. Hell, *ask* was mild—he'd *demand* an explanation.

Brian looked for his hands, realising they were secured behind his back. Thankfully, Ted hadn't tied his legs down. *What in the fuck is happening?* Vomit

157

on his shirt and the floor, shit in his pants—Brian hadn't been in this kind of state since nursery.

He tried to scream—baked air exited his mouth. Brian swallowed, the clicking sound in his throat ringing his ears. His tongue old sandpaper. He kept swallowing, needed to build enough saliva to wet his vocal cords. He strained to move his hands, but the rope wouldn't budge. At least the knot wasn't so tight it cut off his circulation. Perhaps Ted had learnt that trick in his army days. He hadn't mentioned the army, but he looked the type. Whatever, it was all about getting out of the chair. And when Brian did, he was caving Ted's fucking face in.

The memories flooded back, a little at a time. He'd headed towards the forest, twisting his ankle. Ted had yelled at him. But Brian had screamed back, because . . . because . . . Jesus, that sick bastard, he'd been preying on Yuki, taking photographs, and Brian had caught him out. And then . . .

That dickhead lobbed a fucking baton at me.

It had hit Brian in the head. Brian figured he had a concussion, which was why everything caused him such mind-numbing pain, but it didn't explain why Ted had tied Brian to a chair.

Was the IV even for Brian's benefit?

What if instead of fluids and painkillers, Ted was keeping him sedated?

Brian called out for Ted, his voice audible, though nowhere near full volume.

Brian faced the door, his chair in front of the bed. His car keys sat atop the chest of drawers opposite but there was no sign of his phone.

The cunt's nabbed my mobile.

THEY'RE WATCHING

A window lay to his left. Daylight outside. Was Ted out of the house, doing his rounds?

Making moves on *Her*?

What if that was what this was all about? Ted wanted *Her* for himself.

Her would have nothing to do with a sweaty old humper like Ted.

Her would never descend to that level.

Her was a phoenix, rising ever higher.

A tiny spider on the windowsill, carefully spun its web. It walked a lengthy line of silk, dropping underneath the ledge, and crawling back to its starting point, before climbing along the side of the window and spinning another part of its web.

Brian was caught in a web of Ted's making or was it Brian's own? Either way, he sat trapped in a cocoon of silk, as Ted waited for Brian to weaken enough to drain dry.

Brian tried moving his hands, but to no avail.

"Ted! Ted, you evil bastard, get your arse in here. Ted! Ted, you stupid motherfucker."

He called and called, his insults intensifying, goading Ted, threatening Ted, until his voice grew hoarse and weak.

But Ted never came.

TWENTY-TWO

THE SKY DARKENED then brightened, and all the while Brian fought frantically against the ropes binding his wrists. His ankle still stung. Pockets of memory remained missing. The sequence of events bent out of order.

The more time passed, the more apparent it became that Ted wasn't home, hadn't been home, and didn't give two shits about Brian. If Ted had cared even a little, he'd have changed the IV. But instead he'd let Brian fester in his own grime, forcing him to shit and piss himself over and over.

The spider's web now covered the windowsill's righthand corner and had already captured some tasty morsels to feast on later.

How many morsels had Ted captured?

What if this was all some crazy ruse and Ted and the bearded man were working together? Brian had considered the possibility when he'd discovered those photographs—the more he ruminated, the more plausible it became. He couldn't believe he'd almost trusted Ted.

Was he even a private investigator?

"Well, is he?!" Brian shouted, looking at the spider for answers.

THEY'RE WATCHING

Brian would die in that room if he didn't get the hell out of there.

His wrists rubbed raw from the ropes and he still couldn't get his hands loose.

Could he break the chair?

Brian leant to his left. Head fizzing with hot pain. To break the chair he'd need to tip it past its balancing point.

He tried lifting himself but his swollen ankle screamed in protest, and he could barely raise the chair off the ground.

He tried again, then again. Sweat wetting his body. His ankle pleading with him to stop.

Leaning to the right wasn't as painful. He leant as far as he could, and the legs on the left rose. He rocked left then right, left then right.

Wood creaked against wood. The left back leg working its way out of the socket.

Brian set the legs down, standing as high as he could, lifting the chair off the ground. Just as he was about to lose his balance, he slammed the chair hard against the floor and something cracked.

He looked down. Crossbars connected the back legs to the front. The left bar was split.

Brian stood again, slamming the chair down. The back left leg began to give. Fearing he would fall, Brian swung to the right. He leant too hard, watching in panic as the chair tipped and the floor rushed to meet his head.

His collarbone hurt like hell. His head rested against the cold ground, where he stayed for a second, relishing the sensation. The dull throb from earlier cranked up to a heavy boom, reverberating through his skull in an unending cacophony of agony.

All that effort and he'd only knocked over a fucking chair and with it the IV pole. Miraculously, the IV still lay in his arm.

Too weak to stand, tied to a god damn chair on the ground, he called out. "Help! Ted, you bastard, help me."

His eyes watered. He was so fucked, doomed to die alone whilst Ted tried to seduce *Her*.

Brian tensed, pushing with his thigh and shoulder, he slowly slid across the floor towards the desk. When he reached it, he tried sliding the chair legs underneath. *Damn it, too tall.* Even with the chair on its side, the legs wouldn't fit. Sweaty and panting, Brian twisted his torso trying to wedge the chair leg closest to the floor under the desk.

After several attempts, he gave up. A cramp in his side stinging.

Perhaps he could slam the chair legs against the door. Brian scuttled into position. With considerable effort and tight concentration, he forced much of his weight on his uninjured ankle and stood or at least hopped. His body painted with sweat.

Facing the bed, Brian moved backwards as fast as he could. The impact wasn't much, but it destroyed the left back leg of the chair.

If I can break one leg, I can break another.

He slammed into the door once more. His right ankle twisted.

Brian yelped.

It took some time to recover and reposition, after which he used all of his might to ram the chair into the door. For a moment, his vision faded. He paused, panting hard, body in torment, then pushed again, screaming as the front chair leg splintered near the socket. He applied pressure, splitting the seat further.

With a final slam, Brian broke the front left leg, completely cracking the seat. He fell upon impact. The tension in his arms tightened, then released. Brian caught his breath. Sweat dripped across his brow and into his eyes. He struggled to his feet, waves of nausea rising.

Ankle piercing with pain and head pulsating, Brian gathered his strength and lunged back and into the door. The impact separated the slats from the seat. He collapsed to the floor, the rope around his wrists loosening.

Brian wriggled free and scrambled on the ground, close to passing out. His efforts had scratched the floor to shit, deep grooves cut into the wood.

Brian gripped the desk, pulling himself up and to his knees. The IV was still connected to his arm, but the tubing was no longer fastened to the empty bag. He contemplated ripping the IV out but those film scenes with tough guy actors couldn't possibly convey the pain involved.

Brian stood up, fighting the bile rising in his throat. His vision blurred, then cleared. He took a deep breath and reached for the doorknob.

Locked.

What the fuck?

No deadlock to turn, just a knob.

What kind of paranoid fuck has a house full of doors that lock on the outside?

Brian limped over to the window, peering outside. He could likely break the glass but didn't fancy jumping out. The grass below appeared soft but looks could be deceiving.

The window was a last resort. The spider's web had grown to a complex tapestry of silk. The spider continued to work away. "Looks like you've been busy, little fella," Brian said, his voice broken and dry.

He turned his attention to the door. How the hell to open it?

Brian examined the chair legs—most were too big to fit into the jamb, but the left front leg was different, it had fractured then broke. He picked up the splintered leg and directed it towards the jamb, taking things slow, but only got it half an inch in. Brian pushed further and with more force and—*fucking hell!* What little fragment of the leg he'd managed to wedge broke at the tip. He swung the fucking thing towards the door.

Sweating and swearing, Brian examined the gap underneath the door. It was tight but perhaps Brian could slide the chair leg under the door and pop the locking mechanism.

He got on his knees and jammed the leg under the door. It fit but barely. Brian pushed on the leg, wedging it under as much as he could. At first the door wouldn't budge, and the wooden leg bowed in his hands. He pushed deeper, hoisting it up with slow care. The door moved. He kept lifting, watching the door flex. He raised it higher, harder than before, and then—*FUCK MY LIFE*—the leg snapped in half. He fell to the floor.

Ted wanted Brian to die in this room. That was his plan all along. Lock him away and leave him to rot.

Fuck this, I'm not dying today.

Brian forced himself up, limping back a few steps, then kicking the door with his left foot. The kick wasn't strong enough, and he almost fell down.

THEY'RE WATCHING

Frustrated, tired, and ready to pass out, Brian mustered all his strength and kicked the door again.

Again.

And *again*.

His swollen ankle shrieked in protest, and his left foot tingled, but Brian kept booting the door near the lock. He was ready to call bullshit on the whole fucking thing when at last he punted the door hard enough to deliver serious damage.

The lock popped and the door flew open to the landing.

Opposite, the bathroom door stood open. Brian stepped inside. He twisted the cold tap on and sucked down great gulps of water. It tasted terrible, but he didn't care. It was wet and cold, which was all that mattered.

Brian took a breath, drank more, then turned off the tap. He finally saw himself in the mirror. There was a bump on his head, split with a crusty line of blood from where the baton had struck him in the face. Red smeared under his nose, but it wasn't broken. He splashed water on his face, washing away the grime.

He needed to get out of the house as soon as possible but couldn't go around in an outfit that was now comprised of more shit than fabric. Brian stepped out of his clothes, surprised his trousers weren't as soiled as he'd imagined. His boxers told another story. He chucked them into the bin next to the toilet and stepped into the shower for a rinse. There was no time for setting the temperature properly or luxuriating, but with lukewarm water and a bar of plain soap he cleaned himself up as best he could.

Brian changed into a pair of Ted's boxers and the slimmest cut jeans he could find, fastening the belt on the tightest setting. The way the jeans hung, Brian resembled a little kid playing dress up in his dad's clothes, but it would have to do. He grabbed his keys from the bedroom and was halfway to heading downstairs when he remembered the photographs. He rushed back to Ted's room. There was no way he was letting that old bastard hold onto the photos. They were both a violation of *Her* and evidence as to exactly the type of person Ted was. Brian opened the drawer, throwing Ted's underwear to the floor to get to the Polaroids quicker.

"FUCK."

He couldn't find a single damn shot. He tried the top drawer and the bottom but came up empty. Screw it, he couldn't piss about searching the entire house. The fact they weren't there further proved Ted's guilt. He'd been found out and called out, and with a guilty conscience he'd either hidden or destroyed the evidence. Typical crook.

Downstairs in the sitting room, Brian found his phone and wallet, lying on the table as if waiting for him. The phone's battery was dead but Brian wouldn't waste time charging it, not when Ted could reappear at any moment. The front door was locked and this time the sitting room window was locked, too.

Fuck it, he'd head out the back. Marcy trotted over to him, panting and yelping, though there was no aggression to it. She looked as exhausted as Brian felt, and wasn't that just typical—Ted sucking the energy from all he came into contact with.

"I've got to go, girl."

THEY'RE WATCHING

Marcy whimpered, licked her paws, then looked up at Brian with wide eyes as if begging him not to leave. No can do. Brian jumped up, grabbing the top of the fence, using what little strength remained to pull himself to the top. His arms shook, weakened from the trauma and unused to hoisting his own body weight. He started to slip, quickly placing his feet on the fence and pushing himself atop. He tried desperately to cling on to the fence to prevent himself from falling.

But alas, Brian's hands couldn't grip the top of the fence and he fell to the ground on the other side. Marcy's whining echoed from the garden.

He was free at last.

TWENTY-THREE

THE SUN WAS high in the sky and soon Brian's clothes were drenched in sweat. He cursed as he staggered forward—not giving a damn whether Ted somehow saw him walking away. If Ted dared come close, Brian would deck him. Brian didn't care if Ted was bigger or stronger than him. And he didn't care that Ted had likely killed before either. If confronted, Ted would answer for what he'd done. Brian kept to the pavement near the edge of the road, ready to flag down passing vehicles. Brian hadn't hitchhiked before but given his current predicament he'd risk it. And besides, he doubted anyone would try anything—he looked as approachable as the pocketknife-snatching hitchhiker in *Texas Chain Saw Massacre*. Problem was, that also meant there was less chance of anyone actually picking him up. Especially when they smelt him. To describe him as *ripe* was putting it kindly. Well, whatever, there were no cars in sight, which made his odds of a lift zero.

Fifteen minutes later, he still hadn't seen a vehicle. He felt sick and dizzy, so sat down on the roadside and concentrated on his breathing to save from passing out. In front behind Brian lay a straight road, surrounded by trees. He undid a couple of shirt buttons, then a couple more, his chest slick with sweat. Staying trapped in that room, Ted had doomed Brian to die, but at the rate things were going he might die out here, anyway. Why in the fuck hadn't he filled up a bottle of water or scoffed food from the fridge? He brushed the thought away, knowing the answer—he'd had to get away and quickly, so he could get to *Her*. He laughed high and loud into the unfeeling sky. What fucking use was he to *Her* like this? He could barely walk, was hardly able to string a coherent thought together, let alone a sentence, and the way he looked . . . Jesus Christ, he would repulse Yuki. Irreparably turning her off.

He lay down on the pavement, using his hands as a makeshift pillow. Just a few minutes to catch his breath and regain some energy. Thirty seconds into his breather, Brian heard an engine rumble. He snapped to attention, bolt upright, standing so quickly he nearly exacerbated his ankle injury. A red sports car with the top down cruised in the distance, heading straight towards him. As it drew nearer, he noticed all the passengers were lads, in their late teens or early twenties—no seatbelts and clutching cans of beer, save for the driver who kept both his hands on the steering wheel.

"Hey, friends!" Brian shouted, waving both arms enthusiastically.

One kid raised a hand too, and Brian beamed. His rescuers had arrived. He stopped smiling when the empty can of beer smacked him in the head.

"Fuck off, hobo wanker!" the kid screamed.

"Later, chode-stain," another said.

And with that they were gone, and Brian's head hurt even more.

Ten minutes later another car passed, this time no one threw anything at Brian, but it did not stop either.

⟡

By the time Brian made it to the car park he was borderline delirious and mistook a pregnant woman in a supermarket uniform for a parking attendant. He tried explaining his situation, pleading with her not to write him a ticket. She wished Brian a pleasant day before running off. When Brian eventually found his Ford Focus, it amazed him to see there was neither a parking ticket nor a wheel clamp. Brian punched the air and flipped off the 'warning civil penalty notice in force' sign. This was his first bit of good luck in days. Then he remembered what Ted had said, that he'd taken care of it. Was that just Ted talking shit or had he actually helped Brian out with the parking situation? Brian unlocked the car, flopping into the driver's seat, and starting the engine. He put the air con on full blast, its icy waves just about keeping him conscious. The last time Brian had driven this slowly was back in Uni after he'd toked on a joint.

Somehow, someway, Brian approached Pelagic Court without causing a traffic accident. His heart beat faster when he saw *Her*, standing outside the apartment block. He slowed the car to a stop, pulled up kerbside, and watched. God, he'd missed seeing her. Observing her movements and intricacies. Yuki waved her arms around in quick motions. It took Brian a while to work out she was talking to someone else. A blonde woman with shoulder length hair stood facing Yuki, her back to Brian. Was she a colleague? Someone else who liked to dance long into the night?

To be watched? Did they dance together? Brian's body ached with pain and yet magical energy sparked his mind alive. Just seeing Yuki brought him so much joy. She was alive, she was safe, and Ted was nowhere to be seen. The blonde woman though, who could she be? The woman turned. Brian continued to stare. It was only as she drew closer that Brian realised his faux pas. He raised a hand as if that would iron out his mistake and pulled into the car park. As he swung the car round, reverse parking into his space, he watched the woman approach in the rear-view mirror. His stomach turned when he recognised her.

Helen.

Brian felt feverish. If he wasn't careful, he'd trigger another panic attack. He needed to stay calm, to be jovial even, and to think quickly so he could get Helen to disappear as soon as possible. Brian saw the IV in his arm and rolled down his shirt sleeve. He knew he didn't look good, but no way was Helen leaving if she found out what had really happened. He stepped out of the car and turned to Helen.

"Helen, my love, what a wonderful sur—"

The look she shot Brian cut him off mid-sentence. He didn't know what was going on, but he smelt her fury.

"Brian Thomas, where the hell have . . . " But rage turned to concern as she looked him up and down. "Oh my god. Are you okay?"

"No," he said, which wasn't quite what he'd planned, but there was no fucking plan anymore. It was improv, from here on out.

"We need to get you to the hospital," Helen said. She turned to Yuki. "Call an ambulance."

Brian raised his right hand to object, steadied himself against the car with his left to keep from losing his balance. "I just came from the . . . " But he changed tact, tired of lying.

Helen's eyes narrowed. "You came from . . . ?"

"We're all in danger," Brian said.

"Excuse me? What on earth are you—"

"I was kidnapped. Kind of, I mean, it's complicated because I went with him willingly, only I wasn't really willing but I . . . Well, we all do stupid things, don't we?"

"Just calm down. Slowly does it. Now, tell me, what exactly have you done?"

Yuki paced towards them, standing a little back from Helen like she was her subordinate.

"Brian," Helen said. "Tell me what you've done?"

"He caught me at the library. I was looking into things even though he'd said not to and—"

"Who is *he*?" Helen asked.

Brian swallowed.

"We really should let Brian rest," Yuki said.

"What did I say earlier?" Helen said. "Brian, he gets like this but . . . well, I know how to handle my brother."

Earlier? How long had they been chatting?

"I'm . . . " Hundreds of possibilities raced through Brian's mind. He blinked. This scene was wrong. Helen and Yuki weren't meant to be together. Not now. And certainly not here.

"I appreciate you're not well," Helen said. "And obviously something terrible has happened, but to be perfectly honest, I've been here the best part of a week and—"

172

THEY'RE WATCHING

How was that even possible? It had only been a few days unless . . . Christ, just how long had he been out for? He knew the baton had struck him hard, but it seemed ridiculous to imagine he'd been out cold for more than a few hours. Sure, he'd struggled, locked in that god damn room for a day or so, but *best part of a week*? At least it proved Ted's 'three days' deadline was horse shit . . . then again, Brian wasn't so sure that was a good thing. In his state he had difficulty telling left from right, let alone good from bad, and right from wrong.

"How long have you been in town?" Brian asked.

"Five days. That's five days of childcare amongst other things. Thank goodness Yuki was here to help me out," Helen said. Yuki side-eyed her. Brian's bowels gurgled. "I'm just glad I could stay at your apartment so that I didn't have to—"

"You stayed at my . . . How did you even get in?"

Helen cocked her head to the side. "Oh please. You and those snake plants. You're so predictable. I found the spare key."

Brian blushed. Christ almighty, what else had Helen found? Had she discovered the hole? Had she seen *Her* dancing?

"Why did you come down in the first place?" Brian asked.

"Why'd you think? You sent me that text, saying you'd call, and then you didn't, which was very unlike you. Your phone kept going to voicemail and *and* . . . " Helen blinked. Was she holding back tears? "I thought you were dead, Brian."

"I'm sorry."

Helen straightened her blouse. "So, all considered, I'd really appreciate it if you'd have the decency to tell me what's going on."

Brian didn't know where to begin. Wasn't sure when, where, or how this *had* begun. Everything jumbled.

"Go on, Brian. It's okay," Yuki said.

Brian looked to Yuki. As long as she was there, he could do this. He could do anything. "You know the private investigator I was telling you about? It turns out he's in on all of this."

"In on *what*?" Yuki said.

"That's what I'm trying to find out—"

"Private investigator?" Helen said. "Oh no, I'm not happy about that. This simply will not do. If you're in some kind of trouble, you're to go to the police. We don't mess around with private investigators in our family. Who do you think I called when I couldn't find you?"

Sweat formed on Brian's brow.

"You called the p—"

"Of course, I did. What kind of a sister wouldn't?"

"Well, what did they say?"

"Never you mind what *they* said. Quit stalling and tell me what's going on. I mean it, Brian."

He needed to stay composed, to focus on his breathing, the pressure muddying everything.

"Give him time," Yuki said.

"Listen here, young lady, when it comes to my brother—"

"No, *you* listen, he needs space." Yuki glared, shoulders back, head high, as if challenging Helen.

Helen's eyes widened. Brian could kiss Yuki. He could kiss her anytime, but even more so now. How

174

was this strong, powerful woman both a god and an angel? She'd swooped in and stood up for him. She knew exactly what he needed and when he needed it. Yuki had known him a matter of weeks and yet she understood him better than his own sister.

"He had a panic attack the other week," Yuki said, her voice soft candy.

"Mmhmm." Helen sounded as concerned as an absent parent. "You look like you've been in a fight, Brian."

"It was the PI that did it. In the beginning he was my friend, or at least I thought he was. He treated me well, fed me good food, gave me a nice place to stay but when I found the photographs, I knew he was no good."

"Photographs?" Yuki said.

The look of innocence on her face about broke his heart, as if he was the one who'd violated her privacy.

"They were of you," Brian's voice a croak. "I should have taken them the first time, but I was in shock, and . . . Jesus, Yuki, I'm so sorry."

"I'm really not following this," Helen said, irritation scratched her voice.

"The photographs were of Yuki . . . "

"What *photographs*?" Helen said.

Brian's body begged for rest. Mental and physical reserves almost empty.

"Ted, that's the PI, he told me there was someone snooping around the apartments, possibly spying on people, but he was the spy all along. He had these photos of Yuki, revealing photos—photos he had no right to take."

Yuki went to speak but ultimately nodded. It was difficult reading any emotion into her facial expression. Was she mad with Brian or Ted or did she simply accept the situation? As a young, attractive, successful woman, Yuki had no doubt dealt with her fair share of creeps. Perhaps she had a plan. Was biding her time to exact some form of revenge.

"I'm in trouble, Helen. Yuki knows some of what's going on, but not all of it and . . . " He scratched the back of his neck. "Shit, this is hard . . . I've done some things I'm not proud of and yet . . . Look, the more I think about it, the more I reckon I've brought a lot of this on myself. If I just hadn't done the things I've done . . . "

"We can't help you if you don't tell us," Helen said.

"Yes, talk to us, Brian," Yuki said.

Brian's vision hazed, as if caught between wakefulness and dreams. God damn it, he was so sleep deprived. He wanted out, to push past both of them and head inside. To glug some water and lie down if only for half an hour.

"Or if Brian won't then perhaps *you* should." Helen turned her attention to Yuki.

"What do you think *I* know?"

"That's what I'd like to find out. What have you kept from me, Yuki?"

"Look, what I do or don't tell you is *my* business and what Brian does or doesn't tell you is *his* business. This world, it doesn't revolve around—"

"Please, enough with the condescension."

"No, enough with *your* condescension." Yuki cracked her neck to the left, then right. She rotated her shoulders back in circles. Breathed. Smiled at Helen. "We need to help Brian. That's what's most important here." Yuki looked at Brian, no judgement on her face, pure warmth and kindness.

Brian pressed on. "So, the guy Ted told me about, I actually caught him poking around the apartments."

Yuki gasped. *Shit*, he hadn't told her he'd seen the guy.

"Well, I didn't see him," Brian said and felt his knees weaken, he was lying to *Her*. He couldn't do it. "I mean, not properly, cos it was dark and I was looking out of the window, but I got worried. Not just for me but for Yuki, too."

"Such a good man," Helen said.

"Yes, he's a good man," Yuki said.

"A good *good* man," Helen said.

"Such a good man."

"A good man."

"Stop talking and let me think!" Brian screamed.

Helen put a hand on his shoulder. "We haven't said a word, dear."

Brian blinked. The fuck was she on about, *hadn't said a word?* "Oh, hell, the short version is I went looking for the man and the PI caught me in the act. The son of a bitch locked me in a room and I had to force my way out. That's why I'm so beat up."

Helen looked him up and down. "I think you to need to go to the hospital."

"I'll be all right."

"You clearly aren't all right. You need someone to look you over."

"You're right," Brian said. "But I can't go just yet."

"I'm sorry, Brian, but you—"

177

Yuki's hand touched Helen's forearm, she seemed to stroke it, to caress it even, and for a moment Brian was jealous. "I'll handle it," Yuki whispered.

Then she let go and Helen nodded, slowly, as if Yuki had momentarily hypnotised her.

"We should call the police," Helen said.

"Hold up. I thought you said you called the police."

"Oh, I did. Reported you missing and everything," Helen said. "Though they weren't much use. But now we have something concrete. We can—"

"I don't want the police involved," Brian said.

"Brian, these people are clearly dangerous. You've got one guy putting on a front, pretending to be a private investigator, taking saucy photographs. And another doing what exactly?"

Brian scratched the back of his neck. "That's what I'm trying to work out."

"That's not your job but it is *theirs*. You go to the police, you tell them as much as you can, and they'll piece it together."

"I can't," Brian said. "Not at this stage. I just don't know who I can and can't trust. For all I know, the PI is in cahoots with the police. The fact you called the police is stressing me out."

"Well, I'm sorry if—"

"Honestly, Helen, there's something off about this whole town. The best thing you can do is head back to the Midlands as soon as—"

"Not a chance. I'm here to protect you. Which means getting you to a hospital and talking to the police. These are the right things to do. Besides, I have to follow up with the police. You've been through so

THEY'RE WATCHING

much, you're not thinking straight, which is why I'm here. To think for you. Just relax and let me take care of this."

"No." Brian stomped his right foot down. "For the love of God, do not go back to the police. We can't risk it."

"Risk what exactly?"

Brian looked to Yuki for guidance, then to Helen, but no one said anything. He ran his hands through his hair.

"Brian are you having some kind of . . . " Helen started.

He put a hand up in protest. "Listen, the PI knows about you and he knows about Gracie."

Helen crossed her arms. Her eyes darted off to the left, trying to make sense of it. She straightened, let out a breath, and focused on Brian again. "No, no, that's not right at all. Don't be silly, he couldn't possibly."

"This isn't speculation. This is what I'm telling you. He *knows* about Gracie."

"How? I mean, goodness, I've never met the man."

"He knows," Brian said. "I'm sorry. I wish it wasn't true, but he does. He said as much."

The colour from Helen's skin was quickly draining. "When?"

"A few days back," Brian said, though given Helen had been here five days it was likely closer to a week.

"What exactly did he say?"

"That I needed to think about Gracie. Could be it was some kind of threat."

Helen shook her head. "No. Impossible. You must have misheard."

"I'm afraid not. And there's the photos of Yuki, too."

179

"What photos? Where are these photos?"

"I wish I had them with me but—"

"But you don't," Helen said. "You don't have anything. Nothing but stories. Clearly *something* happened to you, but what, none of us really know. Whatever it is, it's muddled your mind. Photographs of Yuki and threats to Gracie? Come off it. And why would a PI kidnap you? Think about what you're saying, Brian."

He looked to Yuki for backup, she looked away. Were they for real? Brian had told them the truth and they were calling bullshit on it?

"I want to speak to this Ted character," Helen said. "His number please." She put a hand out which was odd in itself. If Brian was giving out Ted's number, which he definitely wasn't, he'd read it from his phone. He wouldn't write it on a scrap of paper.

Yuki stepped forward. "I believe Brian."

They both appraised Yuki.

"And you should, too," she said.

"Oh, please." Helen smirked.

"No not 'oh please'. And wipe that fucking look off your face. I'm sick of this high and mighty, holier than thou crap."

"But I—"

"Just *listen*," Yuki said, fists clenched, breathing laboured. "If Brian says he saw photos then he saw photos, if Brian says he was kidnapped then he was kidnapped, and if Brian says there's a man threatening to hurt or do god knows what to your infant daughter then you best bet your and her life that he's not fucking about. Now are you going to stand there, dither-dathering like this is some upmarket restaurant and you've found a fucking pube in your corporate soup or are you going to do your job as a mother—as a reasonable human fucking being—and haul your uppity arse back home to your daughter?"

If jaws could drop then Helen's would have fallen off her face, smashed through the concrete, burrowed into the earth, and fast-tracked to Hell.

Brian was so simultaneously shocked and utterly enthralled he basically had a 'haven't nutted for ten days' erection. Matter of fact, there was so much blood rushing to his horn, and he'd lost so many fluids already, he wagered if it hadn't been for the IV, he might have passed out.

"You can't speak to me like—"

"But I can," Yuki said. "And I did. Now. Do. Your. Fucking. Job."

Helen threw her head back and turned to Brian. "I do not approve of *this*." She pointed a bent finger at Yuki.

Brian fidgeted from side-to-side, his eyes to the floor. "It's not how I'd have put it, but she's right. You have to think of Gracie. We all do."

Helen pursed her lips. "You really think this PI might hurt Gracie?"

Brian nodded. "I do."

Helen fumbled inside her handbag, took her car keys out with trembling hands. "Okay, okay. I'll go b-b-but, Brian, I need you to be safe. I came here to save you and . . . "

She was losing it. She was actually going to cry. Oh Jesus. Brian couldn't deal with that, he had to stop her. "Look, you're a good sister," he said. "And mother."

Helen's lips juggled, halfway between crying and smiling. "Yes. Thank you. Okay. Good." She unlocked her car.

"Promise me you won't call the police again," Brian said.

"Mmhmm."

"Helen, I'm serious, this PI mentioned Gracie's name for fuck's sake. You can't mess with people like that."

"Best listen to your brother," Yuki said. "Tell him you promise. He needs to hear you say it."

Brian straightened.

"Yes, okay, I promise." Helen opened the car door.

"Good," Brian said. "I'll call you tonight. I'll figure this all out and I'll call you."

"Yes," Helen said. "Yes, you will. I'll see to Gracie and you'll call me. And if you haven't called by eleven thirty this evening, then I *will* come looking for you, and I won't be so reasonable."

Helen's tyres screeched against tarmac as she rocketed out of the car park and towards the motorway.

Brian turned to Yuki, not sure if he'd rather fuck her or ask her what the fucking hell she was doing. She was heaven and she was sex, but she was also strong and volatile. She had a wild streak and a real mouth on her. The more layers he unravelled, the more he wanted *Her*.

"So, that," Brian said. "That was something, huh?"

"She needed someone to put her in her place," Yuki said. "And okay maybe I shouldn't have been quite so blunt, but she's been hanging around here much of the week. Gnawing at me. There's only so much a woman can take, you know?"

"She's a worrier," Brian said. "And given what actually happened I suppose that's—"

"I was worried, too," Yuki said. "I wish you'd called me. I wouldn't have known what to do without you, Brian."

If words could kill . . . Letting his sister down was one thing, but now it was Brian who was on the verge of tears, overcome by emotion—to think he might have disappointed *Her*. He'd wondered about calling, letting her know what was going on with Ted, but he'd trusted that bastard, and now it had come back to bite him. He would never keep anything from *Her* again. He made her a silent promise there and then. Better than a promise. A vow. As if joined in matrimony.

Brian placed his hands together in prayer, bowed his head slightly. *I wouldn't have known what to do without you.* Did he mean that much to *Her*? He had to show her how sorry he was, to let her know he never meant to hurt her.

"I was thinking about you *all* the time," he said, staring into Yuki's wondrous eyes. "And yet I didn't call. I've been so stupid. So utterly selfish and wrapped up in my own misfortune. I should have called. You're right, you're so right, you're always right. I have no excuse for not calling and yet—"

"Helen did a lot of snooping," Yuki said.

Brian's stomach dropped. Was his sister a peeper, too? Had she looked through the hole and Yuki had caught her in the act? Had her hands started wandering, the inevitable spell of *Her* forcing Helen to—

"The police really did mug her off," Yuki said, then laughed like it was one hell of a punchline. Brian didn't get it. "When she said she thought you were dead she was being serious. She checked at the local hospitals, too. Even met up with old Pinky at the café." Yuki rolled her eyes. "I told Helen she was overreacting, but you know your sister. At least she cares about you. Anyway . . . " Yuki retrieved her car keys from her pocket. "I have to get going."

It was only then that Brian registered she was dressed up in a black suit with a white blouse. "Oh, Christ. Is today the big day? Your interview with The Dolori Academy?"

"It isn't the interview, but it's related."

Brian waited for Yuki to go on, but instead she unlocked the car. "Your sister won't go to the police," Yuki said as if she knew it for a fact. "But I need you to make me a promise."

"Yes. Anything!"

"I don't want you leaving town. At least, not until I return. No matter how rough it gets, you stay here, so we can sort this together."

Together. Brian liked that. He liked it a lot.

"Of course," Brian said. "*Together*."

Yuki opened the driver's side.

"Wait," Brian said. "You can't go."

"I *can't* go?" Yuki repeated.

"I mean, like I said, the PI, he has photos, it's not safe for you to go off on your own like—"

"*Please,* I can handle myself," Yuki said, getting into the car. "It's gonna take a lot more than a few photos to scare me."

And Brian believed her.

He believed in *Her*.

TWENTY-FOUR

AS SOON AS Yuki left, Brian headed inside to scoff food, glug water, get a proper shower, and clean himself up. In the shower, he removed the IV. It stung like hell and there was a not insubstantial amount of blood. The crook of his elbow and forearm were severely bruised, splotches of yellow in the purple and black. Brian bandaged up the wound and popped back a couple of paracetamols to ease the pain. After everything he'd endured, he'd need something much stronger than paracetamol to straighten himself out in the long run. Brian intended to make good on his promise to Helen to check into A&E and even looked up the nearest hospital on his now partially-charged mobile phone. But before A&E, before anything else, he was heading back to the house where he'd first encountered Ted. The fact Ted hadn't wanted him to go inside, made Brian reckon there was something worth seeing and before any of this bullshit, Lexie had urged him to check it out, too. Brian was going there and there wasn't a damn thing anybody could do or say to stop him.

➳✦➳

MICHAEL DAVID WILSON & BOB PASTORELLA

By the time Brian made it to the old house, the skies were dark, and the moon was just as striking as the previous time he'd visited. There was no car parked outside the place or around the corner and no discernible movement from within the building either. As far as Brian could tell he hadn't been followed and there were no signs he was being watched. Brian reckoned Ted had discovered he'd escaped, which left him paranoid and extra cautious. He'd grabbed a knife before leaving, this time vowing to exercise a little more caution so as not to wind up stabbing some innocent. Not that Ted had turned out to be a textbook definition of innocence, but still. Brian felt for the knife in his back pocket, though honestly, the thought of having to use it scared more than comforted him. He waited a good twenty minutes before approaching via the back garden. This time when his arm stretched through the jagged glass and his fingers found the latch, nobody stopped him from opening the door and stepping inside.

The air smelt of mildew. Brian recognised it instantly, he'd had a mould problem in his previous place. The moonlight afforded Brian a limited view of the room, an L-shaped kitchen surface to the left and a breakfast bar to the right that separated the kitchen from the dining room. No door, just a gap between the breakfast bar and wall. He felt for a light switch and found one eventually, but it did nothing. What Brian could make out was grim, not that the place was a mess or even dirty—aside from the broken glass it was in reasonable order—it was just that everything looked so outdated and neglected. There was an old brass kettle with flame-like rust engulfing the exterior, a seventies-style electric whisk, faded turquoise, with a long cord and its own stand, there was even a meat grinder—screwed onto the side of the counter, looking more like a weapon than a kitchen appliance.

Through the next door lay a narrow corridor that offered three options: the front door ahead, the stairs to the left, or the door on the right. Brian opened the door to the right and fumbled for a light switch which he quickly found. This time it worked. Blueish white light illuminated what should have been a living room but was set up more like an office.

What the hell?

No sofa, no coffee table, no television, no bookcase, no cabinets, no house plants, no photographs, no framed artwork. There weren't even curtains, just a thin sheet of white netting which explained why the light had shone through so easily once the man had turned the lights on the last time Brian had been here. And, in turn, others would be able to see Brian.

Trespassing.

Snooping where he shouldn't.

And why? Because Lexie had insisted? Because Yuki could be in danger or, worse, still *involved*? Because Ted's actions and inactions had left Brian paranoid? He shook his head. Brian was here of his own volition. Because he needed to uncover the truth for himself. This had been his decision, and he had to take responsibility. Whatever happened, whatever he found, it was on him and no one else.

Brian felt uneasy in the white light.

Exposed.

Vulnerable.

He could have turned the lights off, to ensure he brought no attention to himself and the house. But he couldn't, at least not yet. He had to take a closer look at things.

In the centre of the room, on a long oak table, sat six computers—old school tower desktops with bulky CRT monitors. On the faded yellow wallpaper were strange aquatic drawings in red ink. A style that seemed to take influence from both Ancient Egyptian and Greek art. Brian peered at the computer nearest to him—no distinguishing marks or logos to suggest a manufacturer, so it was likely custom-built. He moved the mouse, a loud fan whirred, and the screen glowed to life. The display was grainy and showed a bedroom, an unmade bed, and a bedside table with a lamp—behind it lay a clothes horse, overflowing with t-shirts. In the left-hand corner was a timestamp: 15-06-2017 Thursday 22:18. Brian checked his watch, 10:18 p.m.

It was live.

A click of the mouse and the camera displayed a small bathroom: a shower-bath combination, a sink, and basic toiletries. Nothing unusual. Another click displayed a living room, much like Brian's. Sprawled back on the sofa sat a man with a receding hairline, a can of beer in his hand, watching television.

Brian shifted his attention to the next computer—a quick shuffle of the mouse brought the display to life, revealing a similar picture. Though this time the apartment in question looked more like a show house with only white goods for furniture. The place was unoccupied.

THEY'RE WATCHING

The adjacent computer's images were almost identical. Brian would have thought it an exact copy, if not for the difference in bathroom layout—the bath on the right and sink on the left in one, and the reverse in the other.

As Brian was moving over to the fourth computer, he noticed a flicker of movement on the sixth and final monitor. He shifted his attention to it. The timestamp was different here: 15-06-2017 Thursday 19:02. Today but three hours ago. He clicked the mouse, the video paused, revealing a basic media player and options to rewind and fast-forward the footage. Archival footage, playing on a loop perhaps? On-screen, a guy with a bald head slouched in front of the television, swigging from a can of something Brian couldn't quite identify. Three figures in black hooded robes entered the living room from the right, they snaked behind the guy who sat oblivious on the sofa. Could he not see them, or did he simply not care? Perhaps this was some sort of live action role-playing game, though Brian had never heard of one involving almost all the players in costume and one dude in jeans and a t-shirt. So then, could it be a sex thing? The hooded figures were standing still as statues which didn't seem particularly erotic, but everybody has their kinks—maybe the three of them were just watching, getting off on the guy's ignorance. His *innocence*. Brian shook his head, seemed far-fetched. Definitely not a sex thing. The hooded figures raised their hands, their fingers wiggling in perfect unison as if choreographed. The guy swigged back his drink. Another hooded figure appeared in the doorway, this time from the left. The figure differed from the rest, his robe was blood red and he was much taller.

Holy shit, was this *the* Red Robe? The guy who'd paraded the streets, shaking hands and cheered on by the masses?

This time the guy on the sofa saw. He went to get up, but Red Robe raced forward, pushing him down. The three figures in the black robes lowered their arms and joined Red Robe, boxing the guy in. Red Robe gestured for the guy to rise but he stayed put which seemed to agitate Red Robe. He pointed to the robed figure to the far right, who promptly grabbed the guy's can and flung it across the room. Now the guy rose, meeting with a straight right from Red Robe, then hitting the floor. The figures in black robes picked the guy up and to his feet, escorting him out of the living room.

Brian fast-forwarded, but the room remained empty until the present moment. He clicked again to see if he could access other rooms' archival footage, but if he could the necessary commands and controls were eluding him. He rewound the video, to see if he'd missed anything—perhaps a smile or knowing wink to prove this was a game—but the more he viewed it, the more sinister this appeared. Had he witnessed an abduction? Should he dial 999? He wasn't sure if it would do much good. For one, he had no address. For two, this had happened hours ago. Plus, if he told the police how he'd come to see the crime, he'd wind up admitting to his own guilt for trespassing. On top of all this, Brian wasn't sure there was evidence of an actual crime. For all he knew, it really was role-playing. Better to leave it for now.

THEY'RE WATCHING

When Brian turned his attention back to the fourth computer, his heart rate sped up. The on-screen image triggered a strange sense of déjà vu, as if he knew the place—but how?

Then she entered the room.

Her.

TWENTY-FIVE

BRIAN HAD KNOWN there was something deeply troubling about the man—Ted had called him volatile and highly dangerous—but to think he'd been watching *Her* sent a shiver up Brian's spine. How dare he! How dare he violate her privacy. How dare he see her most intimate moments. How dare he rig up a surveillance system to her apartment.

On-screen, Yuki performed her nightly ritual—her sultry dance—as Brian watched. Even in his current state—beat-up and hurting from the days spent at Ted's—Brian grew incensed that some man, some dickhead stranger, was watching *Her*. Jesus, Ted's Polaroids were tame in comparison. This guy, this flesh-formed parasite, was the worst of the worst. And yet, Brian couldn't tear his eyes from the screen. He felt a little excited. How could he not? *Her* didn't just dance, she created art, and he'd gone without her artistic expression for almost a week. Damn it, she *was* art, and that piece-of-shit man, whose house he stood in, had taken advantage. He'd crossed the very boundaries of human decency. What had happened to the bald guy was child's play compared to this. Brian's hands clenched into fists. He had to get out of there and tell *Her* what was happening. He should never have held things back—should never have left the library with Ted in the first place. Matter of fact, he shouldn't have even gone to the library. He should have taken Yuki and gone far, far away from this wretched town. He'd done nothing. But now he was doing something.

He had to protect *Her*.

Brian looked to the fifth screen, recognised it instantly: his own apartment. He felt sick.

Does that mean he saw me watching Her?

Brian clicked through to the shot of his hallway. So, the camera was attached to the same wall the open wardrobe lay against. Brian breathed slight relief. It would track him entering the wardrobe but once he was inside, *nada*.

His relief was short-lived when he turned back to the screen showing *Her*. The dance complete, she lay sprawled out on the bed, wearing a nightdress that left little to the imagination, and reading a paperback. Brian couldn't make out the title.

This vile wretch of a human being had no right to do this to *Her*. No right at all. This was worse than anything Brian had imagined.

Brian checked for the knife in his back pocket, his fingers grazing the tip. He had to warn her, and fast. He knew what he'd done was wrong—peeping on *Her*—but this was different. This took things to another level.

Brian scanned the room for recording equipment, something he could destroy to protect him and *Her*, but came up empty. No matter. He could return to the house later, but for now he had to get to *Her*. He had to run back through the fields and to Pelagic Court.

He switched the lights off and made his way towards the back of the house. He wanted to leave the place as he'd found it—didn't want to clue the man into him being there, into him *knowing*.

Violating bastard. Her is sacrosanct. Her is . . .

Brian stopped himself, knew how he'd wanted to finish it.

Her is mine.

Her is for me.

For a moment Brian wondered if he was no better than the man, but he brushed that thought aside. Of course he was *better*. He had feelings for *Her* and *Her* had feelings for him. They did things *together*. That's what he'd promised her.

As he walked back through the house and into the kitchen, he paused at the smashed windowpane, looking towards the old wooden swing. He swore he could see something or someone sitting on the swing, rocking back-and-forth—his palms turned to water, his mouth to sand—but as he came closer, he realised that wasn't right. His mind, the excitement of it all—the adrenaline—was playing tricks on him. There was nothing rocking on the old swing. Nothing at all.

TWENTY-SIX

OUTSIDE THE FRONT of the house, Brian squinted into the distance, scanning for danger. He half-expected Ted's BMW or the rusted-out car to screech around the corner, either or both men catching him in the act. Perhaps far-fetched, but they'd both been watching him and *Her*. They were both part of this. Complicit. Brian reached back and felt for the knife, still there. A little piece of protection should he need it. He tried calling Yuki, to warn her ahead of time, but it kept going straight to voicemail. *God damn it.*

Brian walked through the field, stopping every couple of feet to listen and look around. The journey back was easier than the walk getting there—the adrenaline and urgency of the situation, anesthetising the pain. Tall grass rippled like waves in the sea. The moon hung low in the sky, mostly obscured by clouds, but the cold front pushed at them, Brian's visibility slowly increasing. Soon the moonlight would be enough to guide him. He pressed on and soon saw the glow from the torches through the weeds.

When Brian reached the car park, he stopped walking. He listened and looked. The man and his car weren't there. And neither was Ted. Yuki was probably safe.

Probably.

Brian looked to the fish torches, distrusting. Something about them seemed sinister, off-kilter. Perhaps just his mind playing tricks again—the man and the cameras, sending his imagination into overdrive.

Still, better not to take any chances.

He licked his lips and ran through the car park. Getting closer, he noticed all Yuki's windows were dark.

Was she sleeping?

It didn't matter. He would wake her. The sooner she got out of there, the better.

What would he tell *Her*?

With time he'd divulge everything but not straight away. Though he had to explain enough. He needed her to act and *react*—to take him seriously. Brian stood ten feet away from the complex entrance without a plan. All he knew was he had to get her the hell out of there.

Right now.

He quickened to a sprint for the last couple of steps and pounded on her door with his fists.

He listened but couldn't hear anything.

"Yuki," he said, probably too low.

He pounded the door again, yelling her name this time. Footsteps from inside.

"Who is it?" Yuki asked, sounding understandably irritated.

"It's Brian. Please open the door."

He heard the deadlock slide out and the door opened. Her hair was loose, and she wore a thin black night robe. Yuki's eyes widened. "What happened to you? Did you have another run-in with that PI?"

THEY'RE WATCHING

At first, Brian didn't know what she meant. He looked down and saw his clothes. Dirt and dried weeds hugged the calves of his trousers. Dust, grime, and sweat covered his hands and arms. "You've got to come with me," he said.

"What?" She looked at him and smiled, all cutesy. "Isn't it too late to go hiking?"

"Yuki, I'm not *fucking* around. You've got to get out of here, you're in danger."

She stepped back from the door. His words were ugly. Perhaps even scary. He'd lost his temper because he was panicked. Because *he* was scared.

"I'm sorry. I'm not trying to frighten you. It's just, I mean, shit, things are even worse than I thought."

"Is this about that man who—"

"Yes," Brian snapped. "I haven't exactly been straight with you, but the other day I followed him to his house. Then tonight I went back and—"

"You did *what?*"

"I promise I'll explain, but for now we have to go. Trust me, he's dangerous." There was no telling what would happen if they were caught—if those robed figures would rough up a guy minding his own business on the sofa, a trespasser like Brian would get it loads worse. Brian reached for *Her* hand. She let him take it, and he could feel her shaking. "Will you leave with me?" He had no idea where they were going, but outside the apartment was better than inside. To get her away from the man and the torches and Pelagic Court.

To get *Her* to safety.

"You're gonna have to give me more than that. It's late, I can't just go jetting off in the middle of the night because you tell me to."

MICHAEL DAVID WILSON & BOB PASTORELLA

Brian felt tears welling up in his eyes. Yuki was right, of course. He was a relative stranger and yet if she didn't follow him something terrible would likely happen to her. His brain was so fucking fried. "I just . . . " His voice wavered as he struggled to keep it together and there was a change in Yuki's body language as she sensed his vulnerability.

"Okay, Brian, I'm putting my trust in you but if you're messing with me . . . "

Sweet relief swept over him.

"Let me get my handbag." She started to shut the door, but Brian kept hold of her hand. Gave her what he'd meant to be a reassuring smile but in reality was nearer a grimace, as if he was about to throw up.

"Grab what you need. I'll explain everything in the car."

—◦〉|〈◦—

Brian waited in his car with the engine running. After an exasperatingly long few seconds, she finally came, still wearing the robe, though she was now also wearing bright red high-top trainers and had her handbag. She got in the car and fastened her seat belt. "Where are we going?"

"Somewhere safe."

Brian didn't have a clue where they were ultimately heading but he knew they had a long night ahead of them. They'd trek up to Helen's first, collect his sister and little Gracie, so the four of them could hightail it together. He didn't know if the man and Ted were working as one, he didn't know if they knew where Helen lived, but these were risks he was unwilling to take. They'd head to a hotel or guesthouse or even lay low in a caravan park. Wherever they were it would be fresh and unknown. Once Helen's address was in the SatNav, he put the car in gear and sped out of the car park, keeping an eye out for the man and the old banger—paranoid the man was onto him, that he had surveillance inside the house and would soon follow.

Yuki reached over and put her hand on top of Brian's where it rested on the gearstick. He looked down and saw he was gripping the lever tight, his knuckles white and bloodless. He relaxed his fist, letting her warmth calm his nerves. Yuki gave his hand a firm squeeze, then rummaged around in her handbag. She pulled out her mobile phone. "Should I ring the police?"

"No, not yet."

"No?"

"Let me get us settled somewhere safe first, then we'll call."

Though what they'd tell the police, Brian hadn't the foggiest. Was he somehow complicit in this entire affair? Brian didn't want the police to know about his own activities. Though peeping wasn't illegal, was it? There was also the part about trespassing he'd have to explain.

"So, this house, the guy's house . . . well, barely a house, it's halfway torn down, in complete disrepair, though it has power, but, anyway, point is, I was there."

"Where exactly is this house?"

"Past the car park. There's some housing once you get beyond the field."

He could feel Yuki's eyes on him. Knew he was mumbling, talking too quickly, sweat dribbling from his forehead.

"Is that where you were? All this time?"

"No! I was at the PI's, just like I told you."

Brian felt his chest tighten. He trusted her with his *everything* whilst she questioned even the basic details of his account. He would have to do better: no more lying, no more peeping, and no more sneaking around.

"What happened tonight?" Yuki said. "Tell me what you saw, Brian."

He liked that. Every time he heard his name in her mouth, it eased him somewhat.

Brian slowed at a junction stop sign, practically rolling through, looking both ways to make sure another car wasn't barrelling towards them. "I looked in the windows of the house. There really wasn't much to see, but there were computers set up on the table. Surveillance equipment. He was spying on us . . . spying on you."

"Spying? Like, he has cameras set up in the house? Is that what you mean?"

Brian nodded.

"And you looked *through* the windows?"

It was obvious he'd gone into the house, and Brian felt ashamed to say it aloud. At least they were nearly out of the town. Soon they'd hit the motorway, putting them one step closer to Helen and Gracie, at which point Brian could loosen up a little. Perhaps he should call Helen to let her know they were on their way. Give her an update on what had happened. How the situation had escalated. Though he wasn't sure he could manage a coherent enough sentence. It'd come out all panicked, and then what? Helen would panic, too, and call the police or worse . . . No, he'd ring her before eleven thirty, just as she'd asked, filling her in on some of the smaller details, before they turned up unannounced.

Brian took the next right and merged onto the main road. There wasn't much traffic, and it was extremely dark, as if someone had dimmed the street lights.

Brian glanced at the time. They were about an hour out from Helen's deadline. She'd near enough threatened to return if he didn't get in touch. Brian reached for his phone.

"I need to send Helen a text," he said.

"Eyes on the road. Give me the phone."

Brian passed it to Yuki. "Tell her everything's okay and I'll call in a couple of hours?"

Yuki agreed, writing a quick message before passing the phone back to Brian. He let it rest on the seat with him. Helen taken care of, Brian's mind eased somewhat.

Continuing to the right, he followed the road out of town, successfully avoiding hold-ups at several traffic lights. Red flashing lights lay ahead.

Damn, I made the lights but forgot about the train.

Yuki's hands fumbled in her handbag again. She stared straight ahead. Brian could tell she was nervous, even though she tried not to show it. Her mouth set in a grim line. He reached out and patted her arm. "Everything will be fine."

She smiled at him, still looking straight ahead. "I know."

Brian stopped at the level crossing, craning to see how long the train was. It wasn't moving fast, but it was too dark to see where the carriages ended. They were the only vehicle at the crossing. He shifted the car into neutral, applied the handbrake, and leant his head back on the headrest.

"I'm exhausted," he said. "I'm sure you are, too."

"Yes."

Brian looked over at Yuki. Moonlight bathed over her, illuminating her face and hair.

Her face.

Her hair.

Even now, she was the most beautiful woman he had ever met. There was no way he would ever let anything bad happen to her.

Yuki pulled a small handkerchief from her handbag. She leant forward, reaching over as though to give him a kiss. Brian noticed as her robe fell open that she was naked underneath. The moonlight pulsated over her breasts. He moved towards her to meet for the kiss, and she pressed the handkerchief to his face and held it there until everything turned to grey.

TWENTY-SEVEN

FIRST BRIAN HEARD the wind, then the ocean, or what he thought was the ocean, except it sounded as though wads of cotton were shoved in his ears. Someone was laughing and Brian was cold. Lying on his side, he couldn't feel his hands and couldn't lift himself up. It felt as though his tongue had been cut from his mouth. He blinked, but it was dark. Flashes of dark red shuttered across his field of vision. He felt his breath as every exhale blasted back into his face. The red flashes increased in frequency and size, growing larger, as though something was cresting to the surface in a pool of black water. Waves of red emerged from the black, soundless. It was coming closer to him. He tried lifting his head and something, *someone*, held it down. The force was gentle yet firm. Brian couldn't feel his legs. Did he still have legs? Maybe this was his new world, the red and black liquid that reeked of his breath and sounded like waves of cotton. Perhaps he didn't need legs, or arms, or a mouth in this new world. Someone was talking next to him, muffled voices speaking back and forth— one voice deep, the other soft, higher pitched.

Her.

Yuki.

He'd been taking her away, and then she'd held a handkerchief to his face whilst he'd sneezed, only he hadn't needed to sneeze, it had been something else. Whatever it was, it was coming for him, through the red, through the black, through the cotton candy waves.

Hands grasped at his shoulders and pulled him upright to his knees. He couldn't hear the ocean anymore, only the sound of feet shuffling on the ground. He started to fall forward—someone supported him until he regained his balance. Still wobbling, Brian realised falling down was something they didn't want him to do. Whoever they were.

The sound of the wind and the light of the moon ripped through the black and red.

Now he saw.

A man stood in front of Brian, a small cardboard box to his right, near to bursting, hoods spilling out of the top.

A hood, that was what had been on his head.

They hadn't wanted him to see what was going on until now.

Brian looked around. He was right about the ocean. They were on the beach. A large outcrop of rock cast a shadow over Brian, whilst the flames from two lit torches kissed and licked the shadows.

Brian was not alone.

There was the man, of course, but there were others too. The man stood in front of him, wearing a red robe. What looked like a tattoo snaked out of the garment and halfway up his neck. Ink almost as red as his robe. This was the man Brian had seen outside the apartment complex, looking up at *Her* window, the same man whose house he'd entered with all that surveillance equipment. To his left, three men, bound like Brian, with their hands behind their backs and gags in their mouths, knelt in the sand. That was why Brian couldn't feel his tongue. He was also gagged. To his right, another kneeling man. He, too, was bound and gagged. In front of each man stood a woman wearing a black robe.

There was a woman in front of Brian.

He arched his neck to look up at her.

Yuki stared back—her eyes black in the moonlight. *Her*.

The tide was coming in. The man said something in a language Brian couldn't understand and all the women took off their robes. They were naked—the moonlight making their bodies glow. Softly, the man began to chant, and the women danced. Slowly at first, gyrating to an invisible beat driven by the man's low voice. The waves were coming in harder now, Brian could hear them over the chanting. Spray misted his face.

As much as he wanted to, Brian couldn't take his eyes off *Her*. She danced in front of him, just as she had so many times before, only now it apparently meant something.

The man's chant grew louder. He was practically shouting, his voice echoing over the waves, louder and louder, and the waves came in faster and faster.

Yuki stepped forward and placed her hands on Brian's shoulders. He closed his eyes as her soft pubic hair grazed his nostrils, his cheeks, his lips.

He opened his eyes and saw the other women also held the shoulders of the men kneeling before them.

Water lapped at his legs. The tide was coming in, but Brian could no longer hear the waves over the man's chanting. Brian felt a pressure in his chest. Light at first, it turned more painful by the second as the tide came in around them. A sharp pain in his abdomen made it difficult to breathe.

Yuki let go of his shoulders and stepped back, her eyes never leaving Brian's gaze. The other women did the same. The man was silent now, and all Brian could hear was the sound of the waves crashing against the rock.

That's when the screaming began.

The man to his right howled, his voice high and loud. Brian watched as the man arched his back, then fell forward into the sand. His eyes were looking right at Brian but focused on some far-off vision only he could see.

As the man's eyes dilated, a trickle of blood leaked from his open mouth.

He was dead.

The man to Brian's far left arched his back, moaning as pain wracked his body. When he fell forward, Brian could see the whites of his eyes. Blood frothed from the man's mouth, pooling under his head. The pain in Brian's chest was worse now, throbbing.

The man directly next to Brian began to convulse. He fell forward and rolled over on his side, shitting himself in the process. Brian watched as the man stared at him for a second. He was trying to bring his arms forward, though they were still bound tightly behind him. The man strained and Brian grimaced when the man's arm broke from the force, his elbow hyperextended. The man's face flushed red, and a blood bubble foamed from his mouth and popped, throwing sticky phlegm on the sand.

There were only two men left kneeling. Brian could barely breathe. It felt as though metal bands were clamped around his ribcage. He looked at *Her* frantically, his eyes pleading.

She stared back, her face expressionless.

The kneeling man fell over and didn't move. Brian could see his face—he knew this man.

Ted!

They'd roughed him up pretty good. No doubt Ted had put up a fight. His face was puffy and bruised. Brian wondered how they'd gotten the best of him. Ted's expression lay vacant—he was damn near unconscious, oblivious to everything happening around him. Had they drugged him? Forced him into obedience? What if Ted had been right all along? Had intended to remain true to his word and yet . . .

Oh Christ, Ted, what have they done to you?

Blood poured from Ted's mouth. So much blood, much more than the others. Crimson pooled in the sand, a thick line rolling to where Brian knelt. The blood trail slipped under his knees, soaking his trousers. There was so much red, the moonlight reflected in it. Tears streamed down his face, falling from his chin, and mixing with the blood.

He'd never seen anyone bleed like that. Had they poisoned Ted? Would that make him bleed internally like that? Or was something else at play?

Brian closed his eyes, heart pounding, unable to breathe, clenching his muscles in anticipation of whatever was coming his way. His torso and chest throbbed erratically with his pulse. He tried to take a full breath, but only got a little air in his lungs. When he exhaled, his throat wheezed.

Laughter.

Someone was laughing.

He opened his eyes and saw the man in the red robe standing before him, cackling. The moonlight waned as though darkened by clouds, then the sky exploded in brilliant white light. The entire beach illuminated. Waves crashed violently at the shore, sending water high into the air. A rushing sound filled Brian's head, though he was uncertain if it was the ocean or the moon or something his mind conjured up. The man's robe loosened, falling partially open to reveal a full body tattoo—a complex piece with aquatic motifs, not dissimilar from the symbols and illustrations he'd seen in the man's house, peppering the wallpaper in the surveillance room. The man pointed at the sky, at the moon, and cackled with laughter. Moonlight bathed his body. Jumping up in the air, the man landed on his feet, then fell to the ground, laughing so hard he wheezed. Pulling himself up, the man ran into the ocean, leaping into the waves, his red robe flapping in the wind until it hit the water. It ballooned out for a second, before wrapping around him.

The light in the sky dimmed.

Everything returned to normal. The waves rolling in with less ferocity, their crashes on the beach nothing more than slight ripples. Black clouds rolled across the sky, moving swiftly over land.

The other women had their robes back on and were dragging the dead men around the outcrop of rock. Yuki leant over Brian, working her hands behind his back, untying the rope that kept him bound. She pulled the gag from his mouth and Brian took a deep breath. He coughed, clearing his throat. His chest still hurt, but not as bad as before. At least he could breathe.

Yuki looked down at him. The sky turning light— the sun coming up. She started to say something, then shook her head.

"This was all some kind of sick game?" Brian asked.

"Not a game."

"Then what is all of this?"

Her lips formed a thin smile. "You wouldn't understand."

Brian pulled himself up. "Are you going to leave me here? I don't even know what the hell happened. The police will want to know."

"And you will tell them what? By the time they get here, we'll be long gone, and no one will ever believe you."

"What about the man? Is he okay with this?"

"Who the hell do you think's running this? He answers to me."

"But he was watching you."

Yuki laughed.

"So that's it?" Brian said. "Everything was a lie. Our date, everything?"

Yuki stopped laughing. "Not everything."

"Oh, piss off then. Just . . . go. Leave me alone."

She leant over Brian and put her face close to his. "Not everything was a lie. It's better this way."

"What *is* this way? I don't understand."

Yuki stood up. "Maybe you never will."

"What if I had never seen you dancing? What if I had never watched you?"

Yuki smiled. "But you did watch me, didn't you?"

"I was just trying to . . . " But he'd promised Yuki there'd be no more lies and he'd meant it. "I did," he said. "I watched."

"You came here. You watched. You were complicit. You made it happen. You didn't have to look through the hole, but you did."

"Yet you spared me? Left me here to tell everyone what happened?"

This was madness, pure insanity. No one would ever believe it, would ever believe him.

Yuki held Brian's knife high in the air. "What makes you think I spared you?"

He looked down at the red on the ground. Most of what he'd thought was Ted's blood pooling around him wasn't Ted's at all. It was his. Brian watched as the slash in his torso spilt blood down his legs. He screamed, the sound echoing in his ears.

Yuki brought the knife to Brian's neck and drew it across his throat.

His neck felt hot. Fresh blood gushed from the wound, dancing with the red from his abdomen, mixing with Ted's blood.

Brian fell over in the sand and stared up at her, his vision fading. Every time he blinked, it was as though his life was winking out from him. Everything turning to smoke. The last thing Brian saw before his vision shifted to black was *Her* face.

The other women joined Yuki and together they grabbed Brian by the shirt, pulling him towards the old rusted-out car parked in the sand behind the rocks. The man, now wearing old jeans and a ratty t-shirt, helped lift Brian's limp body into the boot of the car. Two of the women went back behind the rocks, covering blood with sand, bare feet kicking dunes. The old car drove across the sand to the beach's paved entrance and parked next to a maroon Ford Focus in the parking area. The two women who'd covered the blood walked from the beach to the cars, taking their seats in the back of the Ford. A smartphone lit up on the driver's seat, the screen showing nineteen missed calls from Helen. One of the women leant forward to retrieve the phone and unwound the car window. She lobbed the handset towards the road with as much care as they'd afforded the men's bodies, its screen smashing on the concrete.

A figure stood on the pavement, away from the cars. She wore a long overcoat and black boots—her pink hair lifting in the gentle breeze. She stood motionless, watching the ocean, the back and forth of the black waves, ebbing and flowing, ebbing and flowing.

Endless.

Forever.

ABOUT THE AUTHORS

Michael David Wilson is the founder of the popular UK horror website, podcast, and publisher, This Is Horror. A professional writer, editor, and podcaster, Michael's debut novella, *The Girl in the Video*, was published via Perpetual Motion Machine Publishing in April 2020, and his second novella, *House of Bad Memories*, lands in 2021 via Grindhouse Press. His work has appeared in various publications including *The NoSleep Podcast*, *Dim Shores*, *Dark Moon Digest*, *LitReactor*, *Hawk & Cleaver's The Other Stories*, and *Scream*. You can connect with Michael on Twitter @WilsonTheWriter. For more information visit www.michaeldavidwilson.co.uk

Bob Pastorella is the This Is Horror website manager and podcast co-host. He is the author of the zombie-western short story, 'To Watch Is Madness' and the novella *Mojo Rising*. His fiction has been featured in anthologies such as *Warmed and Bound: A Velvet Anthology*, *the Booked. Anthology*, *In Search of a City: Los Angeles in 1000 Words*, *Borderlands 6*, and *Lost Films*. Bob lives in Southeast Texas.

ALSO FROM
THIS IS HORROR

They Don't Come Home Anymore by T.E. Grau

Water For Drowning by Ray Cluley

The Elvis Room by Stephen Graham Jones

Chalk by Pat Cadigan

Roadkill by Joseph D'Lacey

The Fox by Conrad Williams

Thin Men with Yellow Faces by Gary McMahon and
Simon Bestwick

Joe & Me by David Moody

ALSO FROM THE AUTHORS

The Girl in the Video by Michael David Wilson
Mojo Rising by Bob Pastorella

Lightning Source UK Ltd.
Milton Keynes UK
UKHW040717090321
380036UK00001B/165

9 781910 471050